DISNEP
TALES FROM
ADVENTURELAND
THE
DOOMSDAY
DEVICE

J
460-3711

Written by Jason Lethcoe
Illustrations by Jeff Clark, Jillian Clark, and Denise Shimabukuro
Cover paint by Grace Lee

Printed in the United States of America
First Hardcover Edition, September 2018
1 3 5 7 9 10 8 6 4 2
FAC-020093-18222
Library of Congress Control Number: 2017963737
ISBN 978-1-4847-8815-8

For more Disney Press fun, visit www.disneybooks.com

SUSTAINABLE Certified Sourcing
FORESTRY
INITIATIVE   www.sfiprogram.org
             SFI-00993

THIS LABEL APPLIES TO TEXT STOCK

DISNEY
TALES FROM
ADVENTURELAND

THE
DOOMSDAY
DEVICE

Jason Lethcoe

DISNEY PRESS

LOS ANGELES · NEW YORK

This one is for Alex.

Chapter One
A Narrow Escape

Andy Stanley ducked sideways as the mummy's rotten fingers slashed at his face, barely missing his cheek. The creature let out a frustrated howl that sent chills up and down his spine.

"No you don't. Not today!" Andy quipped, trying to sound braver than he felt. He thrust his hand deep into his pocket for his Zoomwriter, anxious to show this monster that he was capable of defending himself.

But his trembling fingers came up empty.

Where'd it go? he thought desperately.

The lumbering creature aimed another swipe at Andy's head.

Once again, Andy ducked at the last possible moment and stumbled out of the way. His eyes darted around the torchlit burial chamber, anxious to find some kind of an exit. Spotting a low tunnel entrance just behind a stone table, Andy leapt toward it.

As he ran, he patted his leather jacket's pockets, frantically hoping to discover the comforting shape of his fountain pen hidden somewhere inside.

But once again, he came up empty.

"Nuts!" he growled as he approached a low chamber door. He could sense the mummy behind him now, the shuffling of its bandaged feet moving ominously closer and much faster than he'd have ever thought possible.

Andy crawled through the small cobwebbed opening on his hands and knees. The entry opened up to a dark tunnel with just enough headroom for him to stand, but also with no end in sight.

Andy didn't have time to consider what traps or dangers might be lurking in the darkness beyond. He knew that under normal circumstances, Jungle Explorers' Society protocol would have recommended that the member always move as slowly and carefully as possible when exploring a darkened, unknown passageway.

Especially in an Egyptian pyramid where the builders used magical curses to keep grave robbers from disturbing the dead.

But he was so desperate to escape the mummy's clutches that he hurried somewhat carelessly along in the darkness, trying his best to stay on the lookout for any traps. As he went, he slid one hand against the rough-hewn wall to help guide him along the passageway.

Andy kept his gaze fixed ahead, hoping with each twist and turn of the tunnel that perhaps there would be daylight just around the corner. But at every turn all he encountered was more darkness.

There's got to be a way out of here.

It seemed like the inside of the pyramid was a maze that would go on forever!

But when his outstretched palm finally bumped into a rough wall at the end of the dark passageway, he leapt back in surprise. After all the twists and turns he'd been through, his way was blocked.

A dead end! No! It can't be!

But it was.

And Andy could hardly believe his bad luck!

He ran his hands frantically up and down the wall, hoping to locate some kind of lever or latch that had been installed by the builders, some kind of a secret way to escape. It all had to be done by feel, because he could barely see anything at all.

Come on, come on! There's got to be some way out!

Andy could hear the mummy now, each of its bandaged feet making the sound of a *slip* as it slid over the rocky floor and then a *thump* as it made a footfall.

Slip ... thump ... slip ... thump ... on and on it came,

gaining speed as it lurched toward him from down the passageway that he'd just come from.

He shuddered as he thought back to the decision he had made to enter the pyramid first, hoping to impress the other members of the Jungle Explorers' Society with his courage.

But that decision had backfired spectacularly, with Andy promptly falling down a hidden trapdoor and sliding directly into the mummy's chamber. After hitting the dusty floor, he'd nearly wet his pants with fright when the monster had risen from its sarcophagus, turned its glowing, pale eyes on him, and let out its terrible scream.

And here he was now, in a terrible predicament that he'd never thought possible. He was trapped in a dead end, and if he couldn't find a way out, he was about to become lunch for a two-thousand-year-old pharaoh.

This can't be happening!

After desperately probing along the very bottom edge of the wall, his fingers finally brushed over a small recess. Feeling eagerly around with his fingertips, Andy found something that felt like a rough stone lever.

"*Yes!*" he cried, unable to contain his excitement. The builders had indeed designed the blocked passage as a false wall, something to trap anyone who didn't belong there or know its secret. Because of Andy's recent experiences with the Jungle Explorers' Society, he'd learned that most traps had a solution if a person was willing to look hard enough.

Andy gripped the lever and twisted hard.

Moments later, there was a cracking noise, as if the very bricks of the Great Pyramid itself were breaking apart.

Andy watched with anticipation as a rectangle made up of lines of light appeared between several of the stones, and then, with a loud groan, a newly revealed door swung inward with a loud, echoing *WHOOSH!*

And then, as if on cue, he heard the mummy roar from somewhere behind him.

Andy didn't waste a second. He dashed inside the

newly revealed opening, then turned around and threw his shoulder against the door to close it, pushing as hard as he could.

The mummy was so close now that Andy could see it lurching toward him, no more than a few yards away with its long, rotten arm outstretched and its fingers twisted into a hungry, grasping claw.

Then, just as the withered hand was about to shove through the last crack in the doorway, Andy managed, with a final heave, to slam the rotating door shut.

BOOM!

The sound of its closing shook the entire chamber. Andy breathed a shaky sigh. *Whew! That was scary!*

He wiped his hand across his sweaty brow, and as he did, something fell from his sleeve and plunked onto the floor.

His Zoomwriter.

With a mixture of frustration and relief, Andy bent down to pick it up. How it had ended up in his sleeve, he had no idea. Perhaps when he'd put on his coat that morning it had fallen out of an inside pocket?

"Could have used you back there, old friend," Andy murmured as he put it safely into his front pants pocket. No more trusting his jacket!

The passage behind the door was lit with flickering light, indicating that torches were probably nearby. Then he heard the most welcome sound he could imagine. There were voices in the distance, familiar voices that he recognized!

He'd found his way back!

Kungaloosh!

Andy's pulse hammered in his ears as he rushed down the passage, anxious to be reunited with his friends. He could imagine how concerned they must have been when he'd disappeared down the trapdoor.

"Andy!" shouted Rusty Bucketts when he saw the boy emerge from around a corner. The big bush pilot rushed forward, excitedly clapping Andy on the shoulder with a bone-jarring thump of his meaty, big-knuckled hand.

Andy grinned, then winced and rubbed the impacted

spot. "A handshake would have been fine," he mumbled. Sometimes—most of the time—Rusty didn't know his own strength.

As the group of Jungle Explorers' Society members pressed around him, Andy felt a renewed sense of relief just at seeing them again.

Betty and Dotty, the conjoined twins who were deadly assassins, beamed at him and kissed him simultaneously on both cheeks. Abigail Awol, the daughter of Albert Awol, flashed her beautiful ruby-lipped smile and gave him a friendly punch on the shoulder. (Thankfully, it was the one Rusty hadn't crushed.)

Andy quickly recapped what he'd been through with the mummy, and everyone responded with the appropriate amount of astonishment at his harrowing ordeal.

"Always hated mummies," said Rusty. "Dead things that move around give me the creeps. Give me a ferocious tiger or a man-eating python any day of the week. Much easier to fight."

He raised his glittering hook for emphasis. He'd

acquired it after losing a battle with a terrible many-toothed creature called the Dingonek.

Andy couldn't have agreed more. Supernatural things like ghosts, zombies, and mummies gave him the willies, too!

"You'd better watch yourself, or there won't be enough of you left for even tigers and snakes to eat," said Dotty.

"Yes," agreed Betty. "You've already lost an eye and a hand. Next time it might be your head, Mr. Bucketts."

"I assume that you're referring to this?" Rusty said icily, indicating his hook with a wave. Then his expression changed as he grinned at his shiny appendage. "Actually, I prefer this excellent hook to my old hand. . . . Much more useful. Plus, I've added a couple of modifications of my own," he added with a sly wink at Andy.

"We'd better get moving," said Abigail nervously. She raised her torch in the direction of the tunnel ahead. "Knowing that there are mummies roaming about in here tells me that the sooner we get what we came for and get out, the better."

Everyone agreed. Ned Lostmore, Andy's grandfather, had sent them to retrieve an ancient document, one that their enemies intended to use for nefarious purposes. Andy knew that time was of the essence, for the Potentate, the leader of the Collective, would stop at nothing to get what she wanted.

The group moved slowly down the tunnel, carefully avoiding hidden traps like the one Andy had fallen through by edging single file along the rough-hewn walls.

Finally, after about an hour of traversing the long sloping path, the group rounded a corner that opened up into the most impressive chamber Andy had yet seen.

Andy gawked at the impressive sight.

Another ornately designed sarcophagus, this one much bigger and more majestic than the one that had contained the mummy Andy had encountered earlier, was positioned in the center of the floor.

Massive, carved pillars covered with hieroglyphic

symbols stretched to the ceiling on either side of the stone coffin.

But what startled Andy even more was the fact that the chamber was already lit with flickering torches. There was also a large, ragged hole in the wall, indicating that someone had tunneled into the chamber without regard for the Great Pyramid's history or cultural significance.

And that could mean only one thing. There was only one other group that would be here, and they couldn't care less about the preservation of history or the protection of ancient artifacts.

"They've beaten us to it!" Andy exclaimed. A sudden wave of disappointment washed over him. This wasn't supposed to happen!

"What?" shouted Rusty Bucketts. The beefy bush pilot shouldered his way to the front of the group. His red handlebar mustache bristled as he scanned the room, noting the torches that had been placed in make-shift holders.

"Stones and scarabs!" he swore. "This is bad."

Andy couldn't have agreed more. With a sinking feeling in the pit of his stomach, he knew that they'd suffered a tremendous setback.

Feeling numb, Andy walked over to the sarcophagus and peered inside. The heavy lid had been unlocked and pushed aside. The interior of the coffin contained not a mummy, but a small marble box.

And the box, to Andy's dismay, was open.

"The ancient scroll is gone," Andy said. He wanted to add *and all our hopes with it*, but he controlled his tongue. Instead he turned to the others and said, "Now what do we do?"

Everyone stood in silence for a long moment, exchanging worried glances. The page was from the lost Library of Alexandria, a treasured scroll that had incredibly powerful secrets written upon it. It was irreplaceable.

"Not to worry," Rusty said. "We'll get it back."

In dire circumstances, Rusty usually shared Andy's

grandfather's gift for optimism. Andy wished he'd inher-ited that trait from Ned, but he often had a hard time seeing the bright side. The Collective and their leader, the mysterious woman known only as the Potentate, seemed to thwart them at every turn.

Andy was about to express his concerns when a strange, shuffling noise in a shadowy corner of the room stopped him short.

Oh no . . . Andy thought. The hairs on his arms and neck stood up. He *knew* that sound!

"What was that?" Betty and Dotty asked in unison, turning toward the unexpected noise.

Andy noticed a large shadow creep across the wall.

"We're not alone," Rusty said ominously.

Andy tried to steady his wobbly knees when he spotted the thing that emerged from the shadows.

"Mummy!" Andy shouted.

"She's not here, son!" growled Rusty. "You're in the Society now. Show a little backbone—"

"It found us!" Andy cried.

Then the big pilot noticed where Andy's shaking finger was pointing and his eyes grew wide.

Andy was glad that this time he wasn't alone and had his friends with him. He had no idea how the creature had managed it, but it evidently knew ways around the dead end Andy had left it in and had followed him to this chamber.

The very sight of the thing with its rotten flesh and pale eyes made Andy shiver with fright.

"Everyone get back!" Rusty roared as he pulled his famous sling from his pocket. With a *pop*, the steel ball bearing that took the place of his missing eyeball was in his hand. Seconds later, he'd placed the rubber sling on his hook, creating a slingshot. Then the weapon was loaded and aimed directly at the looming creature that lurched toward them with its hungry, glowing eyes and its terrible claws.

"Not another step, you!" called Rusty.

But if Rusty Bucketts had thought the undead thing would be intimidated by his bravado, he'd guessed wrong. From somewhere beneath the tattered wrapping, a mouth filled with rotten teeth let out a terrible, anguished scream.

And the scream was quickly echoed by a chorus of others.

Chapter Two

Dispatching
the Monster

Andy grabbed his Zoomwriter, but before he could fire the atomic pulse that it contained, Rusty Bucketts let out a bellow of rage. He watched as the pilot drew back and fired the ball bearing directly at the monster.

The bush pilot was an expert marksman, and the metal eyeball flew exactly where he'd aimed.

At first Andy thought that he'd missed and watched with mounting anxiety as the ball flew wide of the stumbling creature. But when the steel ball hit one of the torches that had been placed in a wall sconce by their enemies, he saw the genius of Rusty's shot.

The torch exploded in a shower of sparks and flame, sending burning embers showering down on the mummy. The ancient wrappings were so old and dry that the rotten cloth caught fire in an instant.

As flames engulfed the undead creature, a horrible, unearthly scream filled the air. There was a terrible moment as the monster stumbled around the room, waving its flaming arms in an effort to stop the blaze. But the cry was silenced as the fire did its terrible work, leaving nothing in the mummy's place but a pile of rags and ashes.

"I thought cursed Egyptian pharaohs rising from the dead were only a myth," Abigail said shakily.

"Oh, we've seen our fair share of them," said Dotty ominously. "My sister and I used run into mummies all the time in the Sahara on assassination missions. Desert magic and curses are ever present and quite powerful in this part of the world!"

"Here, I think you might need this," said Abigail after spotting the pilot's "ammo" in the mummy's ashes. She handed Rusty the ball bearing, and after wiping it on his shirtsleeve, he popped it back into his empty eye socket.

"We'd better leave," said Betty. She suddenly looked anxious. "Ned needs to know that the artifact is gone and we're going to have to come up with a new plan to stop the Collective."

As the group made its way back down the sloping tunnel, Andy thought about the implications of the lost scroll.

If what Ned said is right, then finding that page means the Potentate is one step closer to locating and activating the Doomsday Device. I wonder what's written on it.

The group emerged from the Great Pyramid, and Andy hoped and prayed that it wouldn't be too late to stop the Potentate and her evil plan. He'd seen a picture of the Doomsday Device, a terrible clock that had been made by dark sorcery in the Middle Ages, and he could only imagine what it looked like in real life. His stomach churned with disgust when he thought about the drawing he'd seen that showed how, as the hour hand hit each number, a carving on the clock depicted one terrible plague after another tormenting victims.

And if the leader of the Collective had her way, the victims she targeted would be the Jungle Explorers' Society. She'd afflict all of them with unspeakable suffering unless she got what she wanted.

Doesn't take a genius to guess exactly what that will be, Andy mused. There was no doubt about it.

The Potentate wanted every single magical artifact that the J.E.S. possessed.

And Andy knew that with that kind of incredible supernatural power, she could effectively rule the world.

I sure hope you know what to do next, Grandfather, Andy thought. *Because at the moment, everything looks pretty hopeless to me.*

Chapter Three

Ned's Mansion

The ocean waves reflected the fading rays of the setting sun. Gulls circled overhead, calling happily to one another as they danced on a gentle Pacific breeze.

The entire group was sitting on the balcony of Ned's seaside mansion in Oregon, sipping cups of exotic thistleberry tea, which their host had assured them would cure any jet lag they still felt from the flight back from Cairo.

Ned Lostmore, a living, breathing shrunken head, was inside one of the many cabinets that he had placed around the mansion. This particular one seemed to be made of koa wood, a favorite among shipbuilders for its resistance to the ocean elements. It had carvings of giant squids and mermaids around the outside of its glass door, and inside, bobbing on a string, was Andy's grandfather.

As Andy sipped the slightly bitter tea and gazed at the beautiful view, he couldn't help thinking that it would have been easy to forget that their enemies were on the brink of unlocking a Doomsday Device that could threaten the entire world.

"All right, just to be clear—now that the Potentate has the scroll, she has the means to find and activate the Doomsday Device, correct?" demanded Rusty.

"If what the legends say about the weapon is true, then yes. Written upon that fragment of scroll is the secret word that is supposed to activate it," Ned said.

"Do you have any idea where the Doomsday Device

might be?" asked Albert Awol. Albert, a grizzled sea captain, was Ned's oldest and most loyal friend.

"We both know, Ned, that you always have a secret or two up your sleeve," Albert continued with a chuckle. "That is, when you used to have sleeves and wore coats. In fact, where do you keep your secrets nowadays? I'd be surprised if you can keep them rattling around in that tiny noggin of yours."

Ned laughed good-naturedly at his friend's ribbing. "I must confess that this time I'm at a bit of a loss. I have no idea where the infernal machine is located," he admitted.

"Then I guess that's it," said Andy, suddenly feeling miserable. "There's no hope. We've lost."

"Tut-tut, my boy. Remember what I told you after our last adventure?" said Ned.

Andy thought back to his grandfather's words and sighed.

The last thing you need to learn before becoming a full-fledged member of the Jungle Explorers' Society is that we never give up hope. It's as much a part of who we are as saying yes to adventure and staying loyal to our friends.

"I know, I know," Andy mumbled.

But privately, he knew that not giving up hope was the toughest attribute for him to learn. He'd always been a worrier by nature, and deep down, it was hard not to think that impossible odds were exactly what they appeared to be: impossible!

"How do we know that she hasn't already activated it?" asked Abigail nervously.

"We will know," said Ned. "The legends say that the clock on the device runs from twelve noon to twelve midnight. During those twelve hours, if the clock ticks unopposed, that one single day will be the most devastating that we, the Potentate's enemies, have ever experienced. I'm sure that every member of the Jungle Explorers' Society will know when the countdown begins, for it's certain to be most unpleasant."

Ned called to Boltonhouse, his mechanical servant.

Seconds later, the big robot clanked onto the balcony. Andy noticed that the machine carried a rolled-up piece of parchment. When it arrived, the mechanical man proceeded to spread it open on the table. Andy stared down at the drawing of the artifact that he'd seen briefly at the Potentate's hideout, a schematic that displayed the ominous clock known as the Doomsday Device.

"As you can see," said Ned, "this is no ordinary clock. The pictographs displayed where each number would normally be indicate the tortures that the victims will endure once the device is activated."

The entire group stared down at the skeletal figures pictured on the clock's face. Each one seemed to be writhing in a different form of pain and torment. Andy had seen it before, and it was even worse than he remembered.

To Andy, it seemed as if each number created something worse for the victim until midnight. At that point,

Doomsday Device? I assume it must have been some kind of very sick and twisted individual," said Rusty.

Ned nodded. "It was indeed," he said. "The creator was a dark sorcerer from ancient times. His name is forgotten now to all but Patrick himself. Leprechauns are known to live a long time; some say about two hundred years is the maximum. But Patrick . . . if the stories are true, then he's been around for more than a thousand years. Imagine that!" said Ned.

"Leprechauns . . . wait a minute, are you talking about the little people?" asked Abigail. "You mean . . . like . . . fairies and mythical creatures like that?"

"Precisely," said Ned. "Remember, not all myths are untrue. Most of those who study ancient lore believe that Patrick Begorra is the last living leprechaun, a magical being of great power and importance. The Eternal Tree is not on any maps, and he intends to keep it that way for fear of someone destroying it."

"Corn and crawdads!" bellowed Rusty. "Then how are we going to find it?"

Andy thought that if a shrunken head had shoulders, Ned would have shrugged.

"No idea, my good man. It's going to take a tremendous amount of luck. I only know about Patrick through legendary stories that I heard while on an adventure in Ireland. I was busy finding a new location for the Blarney Stone, a very powerful artifact . . ." he began.

"Wait a second," Andy interrupted. "I've seen photographs of the Blarney Stone, and it's still on public display."

Ned laughed. "You don't think that's the real stone, do you? Such an artifact is much too valuable to have tourists kissing and slobbering all over it all the time. I swapped it out so that it could be kept safely away from those who would use its magic for nefarious purposes."

"But you still haven't answered the question," said Dotty, returning to the subject. "How do we start looking for this Patrick Begorra? It sounds incredibly difficult to find him if he lives in a mythical, magic tree."

Ned chuckled. "Nearly impossible! Doesn't that make it fun?"

The shrunken head gazed out of his glass cabinet at the horizon. The sun was sinking now, and the sky had turned from bright orange to a dull, ominous red. "There is only one person I know of who might have an idea of where to start looking for Patrick Begorra. He is the foremost expert on ancient lore and has spent much time researching the *fair folk*, as the locals refer to them."

Ned turned his gaze back on the others, his eyes twinkling. "He also has a small but lucrative business creating lightning rods. And he believes, among other things, that he can control the weather."

"Sounds like a nutcase," said Betty.

"Many think he's quite insane," agreed Ned. "But he was present at my funeral, and that alone shows his loyalty to our cause."

Andy flashed back to the day a few months ago when he'd thought his grandfather had died—something that had been designed as a clever ruse to throw the enemies of the J.E.S. off their scent while they looked for the Pailina Pendant. At the time, Andy had known nothing about the ruse. He'd had no idea that his grandfather was in fact alive—as a living, breathing shrunken head!

All he had known was that at the funeral he had encountered some of the strangest people that he'd ever met, though he now called some of them his closest friends. And there had been one who stood out from the rest: a strange wild-haired man who wore a hat and long cloak and carried lightning rods around in a big sack—lightning rods that had bizarre magical symbols forged onto their tops.

"Nicodemus Crumb?" asked Rusty with a bewildered expression on his face.

Ned nodded and gave the bush pilot a piercing look. "Yes, Rusty. Nicodemus Crumb." Ned turned his attention back to Andy and added, "And in the meantime, we'll need to entrust our young Keymaster here with the most important task of all."

Boltonhouse clanked over to Andy and stretched out his metal hand. There was a very ordinary-looking key in it.

"What does that open?" asked Andy.

"It is the key to my mansion," said Ned. "And, more importantly, it is also the key to the vault that lies beneath it. Inside that vault are some of the most dangerously powerful artifacts we have in our possession. The Potentate will no doubt try everything in her power to force us to give it to her. It will be your responsibility as the Keymaster to keep it safe."

Andy stared at the plain-looking key. His stomach churned with anxiety at the thought of so much responsibility. "But wouldn't it be safer here with you?" Andy asked.

Ned shook his head. "I feel fairly certain that the Potentate will eventually attempt an attack on the mansion to try to figure out where our artifacts are hidden. Especially when she finds that, Doomsday Device or no, our stalwart Society won't succumb to her tortures. Albert, would you be willing to stay back and help me defend the mansion?"

Albert nodded grimly. "No need to ask, old friend. Of course I will."

"Torture? Bah!" Rusty exclaimed. "There's no torture in the world that would ever make me turn traitor on the Society." A chorus of voices echoed his statement.

Ned nodded and glanced around the room. "I don't doubt you, my friends. But we also have no idea what dark tortures this clock will release. There might be pain that's so intense, it could change even the most coura-geous of heart. The good news is that without that key, she will never be able to get into the vault. I can safely say that I'm one step a-*head* of her in that regard!" Ned chuckled at his pun, but nobody else was in the mood to laugh.

Ned looked kindly at Andy. "Besides, I can think of no safer place than your capable hands for our most important key, Grandson. Taking it with you on your quest might mean we can keep her at bay a bit longer.

Even if, by torture, some members of the J.E.S. were to tell her about the vault, the fact that the key is far from here will cause her no end of frustration."

Andy's hand shook as he reached out and took the key from the robot's hand. He could feel the solemn stares of everyone in the room as he placed it on his key ring.

"I'll try not to let you down," Andy said, hoping he sounded braver than he felt. And even though he felt several reassuring pats on the back from his friends, it didn't do much to still his rapidly beating heart.

It's all riding on me now, he thought as he pocketed the key. And with that knowledge, he also couldn't help wondering if his grandfather had made a terrible mistake.

Chapter Four
Finding Crumb

It was a ramshackle building made of logs and held together with rope. The sign that read SOUTH SEAS TRADERS was as dilapidated as the rest of the building, and the overall appearance wasn't particularly welcoming to visitors. It was the kind of place that someone had to *know about*, a place that reminded Andy of the speakeasies he'd heard about in cities like Chicago. They were the kinds of disreputable spots that could be accessed only with a password or a signal of some kind.

It had taken just three days to get to the jungle outpost thanks to one of Ned's miraculous inventions, a submarine that was faster than the fastest yacht. And if it hadn't been for his canteen filled with thistleberry tea, Andy would have found all the travel he'd been subjected to lately completely exhausting.

When they'd arrived in the Caribbean, Andy was immediately reminded of all the pirate stories he'd ever read. Swaying palms rocked back and forth in the tropical breeze. The air smelled of brine, and the salt spray stung his cheeks.

For Andy, the exotic beaches had conjured up images of buried treasure, buccaneers, and ne'er-do-wells. If the stories about them were true, then hiding behind the tall palms and glittering coastline were also darker secrets . . . things "dead men told no tales" about.

Thinking about that had reminded Andy that the crystalline beauty he saw all around him might be deceptive and that he should certainly stay on guard for any signs of trouble.

The group had shouldered their packs and made their way up the beach and into a thick grove of jungle plants and heavy forest. Andy's pack was fairly light. Though he'd insisted that he could carry more, Rusty had taken the bulk of the supplies, claiming they weighed less than a feather.

The big pilot was strong, but he'd taken on more than his fair share of the load. Andy had suspected he would be feeling it by the time they reached their destination, which Ned had told them was several miles into the jungle.

The hike had been long and arduous. Betty and Dotty led the way with two very sharp machetes that they'd used to hack and chop a trail for the others to follow. Rusty had followed behind them, red-faced and sweating, but he also hadn't complained a single bit. The experienced bush pilot's lantern jaw had simply jutted forward like the blade of a plow, and he had plunged resolutely after the twins.

Andy and Abigail had brought up the rear. And

unfortunately, all the ruckus they caused as they hacked through the underbrush had shaken many insects out of their nests. Both he and Abigail had spent over an hour swatting and slapping at their arms and cheeks, feeling fairly miserable and each hoping quietly that the miserable trek would soon be over.

They finally emerged into the middle of a small village that Andy had felt certain was not on any maps. Looking around, he saw to his left a small, run-down restaurant with a shingle carrying the faded image of a Bengal tiger. The grimy cook positioned outside was serving up skewers of spiced, sizzling meat on a rusty grill. He caught Andy looking at him and grinned, displaying rows of missing teeth. In spite of the cook's appearance, whatever he was cooking smelled delicious, and the scent made Andy's stomach rumble.

Andy hoped it wasn't tiger. He'd feel terrible about eating a barbecued cat!

Across the way from the barbecue stood a small

wooden dock. There were a few more weathered buildings positioned near it, nestled on the banks of a winding brown river. Andy noticed that one of the buildings was called the Skipper's Canteen and seemed to be a restaurant. Judging by its position, it was in direct competition with the owner of the barbecue across the way.

Where the rustic meat griller was offering simple jungle fare, the Skipper's Canteen looked like the sort of place that was trying to offer a bit of sophistication to the more discerning traveler. The exterior was designed in the French colonial fashion with pink gables and shuttered plantation-style windows. It was strangely out of place in the middle of the jungle and had obviously been built for special clientele.

Andy felt a strong urge to explore everything he saw. He wondered how this whole place had originated. And, more importantly, how soon could he get one of those skewers of sizzling meat at the barbecue?

"So what now? Should we knock?" asked Abigail,

indicating the chipped green door in front of South Seas Traders.

"We could do that, or we could get lunch," said Andy. "I'm really getting tired of thistleberry tea and sandwiches. Anybody else want to try what that guy is cooking?" He nodded toward the ramshackle barbecue.

Betty and Dotty wrinkled their noses. Abigail shook her head. Rusty clapped Andy on the shoulder and said, "I'm in. Always up for some exotic jungle fare." As he and Andy headed over, Rusty added, "I hope they have pomegranate piranha juice. I haven't had any of that since I crashed my plane here in '26."

The women rolled their eyes and followed. "Always thinking with their stomachs," said Betty.

After Rusty and Andy each purchased one of the rather suspicious skewers and Andy had been assured that it was *definitely not* made of Bengal tiger, the entire group approached the door of South Seas Traders and knocked.

There was the sound of scuffling and a few loud

coughs. After a moment or two, a thin, raspy voice called from behind the door, "Why did the elephant quit his job?"

Andy was momentarily confused. *What?*

But then Abigail snapped her fingers and said quietly, "I remember the answer!" Turning to the others, she said, "It's the first part of a password my father taught me when I was little. He said someday I might be asked the first part and that I should answer it if I wanted to prove I was trustworthy."

Turning back to the voice behind the door, she said, "Because he was tired of working for peanuts," finishing the groaner joke.

Andy guffawed, almost spewing half-chewed bits of meat all over the porch. The rest of the group politely ignored him as the sound of several locks being fumbled open came from behind the door before it swung inward with a loud creak. Then the four were taken aback by the appearance of the long-haired, raggedy person who stood in front of them.

"Ned sent us," Dotty began hesitantly.

Nicodemus Crumb grinned, exposing a row of crooked yellow teeth. "Of course he did. And to what do I owe this most unexpected of visits?" He raised his shaggy gray eyebrows in question. To Andy he seemed even more craggy and weathered than he'd been at the funeral.

"We've . . . mmm . . . come to find out about Patrick Begorra," said Andy with his mouth full.

Crumb glanced up and saw that the boy held a skewer of barbecued meat in his hand. He nodded approvingly. "You picked a good day to come," he said. "Old Boney only cooks roasted iguana brains on Thursdays."

Andy paused his chewing, his eyes wide with disbelief. "I thought it was chicken," he managed after gulping it down.

Rusty sidled up beside him, laughing at his surprised expression. "If you're not going to finish that . . ." he said, removing the rest of the skewer from Andy's hand and snarfing down the last bite of barbecue with an appreciative smack of his lips.

Crumb cackled. "Come in, friends, come in. I haven't had any J.E.S. members stop by in a long time." He gestured for the group to follow him, and Andy noticed that he still walked with the slight limp on his peg leg. As if reading Andy's mind, Crumb continued, "Oh, and watch your step. I keep a pet python near the door. Monty's usually friendly."

The barbecued meat lurched uncomfortably in Andy's stomach as he stepped through the door. Looking down, he noticed the pet Crumb had mentioned, a gargantuan green reptile with bright yellow eyes.

"Nice, snake. Niiice snake. I'm not going to hurt you . . ." Andy said quietly, effecting the most soothing voice he could. The truth was, if he admitted it to himself, Monty looked like the only one between the two of them capable of doing any "hurting."

Andy carefully sidestepped around the huge serpent and was thankful that it didn't seem that interested in him. Then he found that he'd walked into one of the strangest and most exotic shops he'd ever seen.

In fact, it was so interesting that he momentarily forgot about his upset stomach.

He gazed around at the incredible spectacle that surrounded him, taking in the high shelves crowded with valuable antiques and glittering treasures. The store seemed to go on and on for miles with row upon row of everything a traveler could possibly need for any major expedition, from jungle safari helmets to Himalayan climbing gear.

Andy whistled softly through his teeth.

"Welcome to the largest bazaar west of the Nile! Or east. I never was much good at geography," confessed Crumb.

Rusty picked up a large lightning rod from an umbrella stand that contained several others. The top of it was decorated with a metal eyeball.

"Ah! Don't touch that one!" shouted Nicodemus

Crumb as he rushed over to where Rusty was standing. He grabbed the lightning rod from the pilot and placed it carefully back among the others.

"Why not?" grunted Rusty, evidently annoyed.

Crumb glared at the pilot. "That's the Rod of Ever Seeing. You've got to prepare before you use it. Takes weeks. Months, even! If you're not ready, *BOOM!*" The old man gestured frantically through the air. "You wouldn't survive the lightning! You'd never gain the second sight! You'd be fried—like those iguana brains you were chowing down on a minute ago! Lightning can travel right through the roof, you know." Nicodemus Crumb's voice had risen to a shaking fever pitch and he wagged an admonishing, bony finger at Rusty.

Rusty snorted and moved over to another part of the shop to examine the other wares. Andy could tell from his expression that he thought the old man was completely off his rocker.

Andy was examining a particularly interesting set of

binoculars that had three lenses rather than two when he heard Betty say, "Mr. Crumb, we've been sent on some fairly urgent business."

Crumb paused in his careful rearranging of the lightning rods. "Yes, yes . . . get to it, then. Why does Ned need to know about Patrick Begorra? I don't owe him any more favors. After all, I officiated his funeral just as requested, although a certain grandson upset what could have been a spectacular storm summoning." Crumb shot Andy a meaningful glance.

Andy cleared his throat and pretended not to notice. He was embarrassed by the memory. At the ceremony, he'd been so nervous that he'd managed a spectacular feat of clumsiness that nearly burned the entire mansion down.

Betty and Dotty exchanged glances. Dotty hesitated and then continued, saying, "Ned thinks that Begorra is the only one who can help us stop the Doomsday Device."

"The Doomsday Device!" Crumb shouted. "What

could you possibly want with the Doomsday Device?!" The old man was obviously very upset at the mere mention of the cursed artifact.

"Mr. Crumb . . . hold on. Settle down!" Andy urged. "We don't want it for ourselves. Our enemy, the Potentate, is going to use it against us. We only want to stop it."

The old man gazed at the group with a horrified expression and croaked, "There's no way . . . to stop . . . the Doomsday Device. Once it's been activated, you might as well give up."

Chapter Five
A Rocky Start

"We're not quitters, Nicodemus," growled Rusty. "The fate of the world is at stake!"

Crumb shot Rusty a baleful glare. Rusty continued, trying to sway the old man to their side. "The Potentate intends to use the Doomsday Device to torture the J.E.S. into disclosing the location of all our hidden artifacts. If the Collective gets their hands on those powerful objects, then the entire world is doomed! Young Andy here is the new Keymaster. He holds the key to Ned's mansion, and the Potentate will stop at nothing to get it."

Crumb's lips moved soundlessly for a moment while he processed what he'd just heard. "A key, you say? Ned's mansion? Exactly what else does it open, boy?" He edged closer and stared at Andy. "It's a valuable key, eh? I'd wager so, if the Potentate wants it that badly. . . ."

Andy felt offended. "Excuse me, Mr. Crumb, but I don't think that's any of your business."

But Crumb didn't seem to be listening. He waved his gnarled hand in irritation and growled, "So that's why you're looking for Patrick. You think he'll help you destroy the clock."

Everyone nodded. Crumb stared at the floor for a moment. Andy thought he looked like he was trying to think of any possible way to avoid helping them. But in the end, the old man's shoulders sagged and he seemed resigned to his fate as he sank into a chair.

"The legends say that Patrick Begorra is an ancient spirit . . . he's also known in Gaelic as the Gille Dubh. I've spent a lifetime trying to figure out where his tree is located. Some say it's filled with leprechaun gold, but that's hogwash. . . . The only magic the oldest tree on Earth truly possesses is to give anyone who knows how to tap into it *eternal life*."

Andy gaped at the old man. His mind boggled as he thought of the possibilities. *Eternal life? That's incredibly powerful magic!*

No wonder Patrick had been around when the Doomsday Device was invented in the Middle Ages! The tree he lived in had magically given him an exceptionally long existence.

Crumb continued, saying, "Anyway, you'll never find Begorra. I tried and ended up lost in the jungle for weeks. No tree. No nothing." He looked bitterly around his ramshackle shop. "I can barely keep my doors open. Do you know how few adventurers come through here these days? If I'd found the secret to eternal life, just imagine the profit I could have made!" Crumb's face twisted into a bitter scowl. "Anyway, trust me—if Patrick really does exist, he doesn't want to be found," he added.

"But let's say we *do* find him," said Betty. "Is there anything we should say or do to gain his trust?"

Crumb narrowed his eyes, fixing her with a grim stare. "If by some impossible chance you did, then all the legends say that you'd have to endure three tests before you could request anything from the leprechaun. Each of them evaluates a person's character, determining his or her worthiness to know the secret of the tree and the treasure it contains."

Crumb held up a finger as if he were lecturing a class. "The stories say that Patrick is a gentle soul, but that you're doomed if you fail the tests. Most of the ancient legends mention the tests involve something called the 'high seas.' For years I thought that meant they had something to do with the ocean and boats. An idiotic notion!"

He waved his hand in irritation at the memory as if trying to brush it away. "Later I found another document that better explained what that meant. It had nothing to do with the 'high seas'—it's actually the 'high

Cs': characteristics that 'high,' or noble, people would have. The Cs are courage, cleverness, and compassion. These traits must be present in the seeker, or he or she will ultimately fail and be destroyed."

Crumb wrung his wrinkled hands, looking troubled. "Took me twenty years to figure that one out. And I still don't know as much about Patrick or the tree as I'd like to. . . ."

The old man trailed off, lost in thought with a wistful expression on his gnarled face. Then, snapping out of his reverie, he glared at the rest of the group. "My advice is that you forget about the whole thing. I wasted too many years trying to find it."

However, after noticing their fixed and determined expressions and that nobody moved, Crumb sighed, then staggered to his feet and said in a dull, resigned voice, "Since you won't listen to reason, and out of respect for Ned Lostmore, I'll help you get to the starting place where legends say the path to the tree is located."

He removed a boatswain whistle from a leather thong

around his neck and blew a shrill note. Moments later, someone emerged from the back of the shop.

Andy was startled to see the huge mountain of a man stride purposefully toward them. If Andy had to guess, he'd say the giant was nearly eight feet tall. He had an oblong face with high cheekbones, and his eyes were covered by small round spectacles that had darkened lenses, giving him a very mysterious air. Andy noticed that he also wore a long black coat that nearly touched the floor—a huge amount of material to cover someone so large.

Nicodemus Crumb nodded at the giant in silent greeting before turning to the group and saying in a gruff voice, "This is Zeus. He'll take you to the boat."

Crumb gave no explanation of who the giant was and didn't say good-bye before turning abruptly on his heel and marching to the back room of the bazaar. Andy didn't have a chance to thank the grizzled old man, for he disappeared behind a door with a slam that set nearly every artifact in the shop quivering.

Andy gazed up at the giant. He didn't know whether he should trust this unusual person or not.

"Follow," Zeus rumbled. His voice sounded to Andy like boulders being scraped together. Everyone, including Rusty, did as he said without a word, and moments later, they had exited the shop and walked across the dirt road. Soon Andy found himself standing at the river dock next to a large, rickety boat.

"Inside," Zeus commanded.

And with a fluttery feeling in the pit of his stomach, Andy, seeing no other option, entered the cabin of the old ship.

Chapter Six

Juju

The ship was a dilapidated Chinese junk. It had reefed sails made of giant canvases stretched over thin wooden spars. To Andy, they resembled gigantic scarlet fish fins.

The smoky cabin belowdecks was filled with pungent incense that had a rather oily smell. The source of the fragrance was dangling pots held in place by brass hooks shaped like dragons. The portholes on either side of the ship were so dark with grime that they appeared opaque, but the rest of the ship seemed fairly clean and was decorated with worn pink silk cushions arrayed on wooden benches.

Nobody spoke a word as they all sat down. It seemed to Andy as if everyone was filled with the same sense of foreboding he felt. He couldn't put his finger on why, exactly. After all, he'd faced many terrible dangers during his previous quests.

But there was something about Nicodemus Crumb that made him anxious. Even though the old man had agreed to help them, something about his manner bothered Andy and made him wonder if Crumb really could be trusted.

Zeus's huge booted feet thudded down the steps into the cabin. The giant walked past them and didn't speak as he busied himself with something in the galley. After a moment, Zeus reemerged from the ship's kitchen with a clay pot filled with tea and several tiny cups.

He silently offered each of them the drink. And after each one of them held a cup in his or her hands, he then raised his own . . . apparently indicating that each of them should follow his example.

Almost as if he were suggesting a toast, thought Andy.

When everyone's arms were raised, the giant said in a low, rumbling voice, "Drink."

Andy took a sip. The tea was very bitter and unpleasant. He had expected something like oolong or jasmine because of the Chinese ship, but he was sorely disappointed.

"Worst stuff I've ever tasted," said Rusty in a low voice, speaking aloud exactly the same thought Andy was thinking.

Ned's thistleberry tea tastes incredible compared to this, Andy agreed silently, grimacing.

Zeus ignored Rusty's outburst and moved to a bulky wooden cabinet with jade inlay that crouched in the corner of the cabin. Andy watched as he fished a small key from under his long cloak and unlocked a tiny padlock on its outer door.

Inside was a small, sinister-looking chest. Andy could tell in an instant that it was something that should probably not be opened. Black skulls were raised all over the lid, and the hatch that held it shut appeared to be made of a finger bone. Andy distractedly hoped it wasn't a human's.

The giant walked directly over to Andy and, after turning the bone latch and opening the lid, said, "Keymaster."

"What?" asked Andy.

Zeus pushed the chest toward him.

"What should I do with it?" Andy asked, feeling confused.

"I think he wants you to reach inside," offered Abigail.

Andy wasn't too comfortable with the idea, considering how wicked the chest looked. But when he tried to peer over the side of the box to see what was inside, the giant lifted the box higher so that he couldn't peek.

Andy gave Zeus a searching look. He really didn't feel

that he could trust him. But since his grandfather had told them to meet with Nicodemus Crumb, evidently he knew what was best.

Andy sighed.

Here goes nothing....

He reached inside the chest and carefully felt around. His fingers brushed some hard objects, but he couldn't tell by feeling what they were. He decided to grasp one of them and was surprised when he lifted out a small, ornately carved necklace.

"What is it?" asked Abigail.

"I . . . I'm not sure," said Andy, examining the necklace closer. It looked like a piranha with very sharp teeth.

"Piranhahaha juju," said Zeus.

"Piranha," repeated Andy.

"No. Piranhahahaha," said Zeus.

"'Hahaha'? Like laughing? I don't get it. . . ."

Zeus held up a long bony finger. "One use."

"One use? What do you mean? How am I supposed to use it?" asked Andy.

But Zeus ignored him and moved on with the chest, offering it next to Abigail. She reached in (albeit reluctantly) and pulled out a different necklace. Andy saw that this one was fashioned in the shape of a parrot.

"Birdcall juju," said Zeus. "One use."

Abigail looked at it but didn't say anything. To Andy, it seemed like she was resigned to whatever was happening and was going to follow wherever this strange set of circumstances was leading them.

Zeus repeated the ritual with Rusty and the twins. Rusty received the "elephant juju," which the giant said was for tracking, and the twins received "discovery juju" and "knowledge juju," necklaces that bore a carved tree and a strange all-seeing eye. Zeus indicated to all of them, as he'd done with Andy, that each juju had one use.

Whatever that means, thought Andy.

He yawned.

The room was feeling stuffy, and the incense seemed thick and oppressive. He'd been feeling alert just five minutes ago but was suddenly starting to feel sleepy. *I really could use some fresh air,* he thought.

Zeus closed the lid on the chest and replaced it in the cabinet. Then he turned to the group and said the most words he'd spoken so far.

"To walk the path of life you must first walk the path of death. This is the beginning of that path," he rumbled.

Andy directed his sleepy gaze at Rusty. None of what the giant said was making sense. He watched as the pilot seemed to wobble where he sat. Rusty's face was pale and drawn with anger.

"What . . . did you . . . put in that blasted . . . tea . . . ?" he managed. Then the big pilot toppled onto his side, landing with a hard thump on the wooden bench. Betty's and Dotty's eyes were already closed, and Abigail was lying beside them. Andy tried to fight the feeling of fatigue that was washing over him but felt himself sliding inexorably toward oblivion. As his eyes closed and gray mist filled his vision, he caught one last sight of the giant looming over where Rusty was lying, apparently unconscious.

"I'm truly sorry, but I never said it was tea," Zeus said.

And then the world as Andy knew it faded away.

Chapter Seven
Trapped!

The first thing Andy noticed when he woke up was that his wrists hurt. He gazed around the incense-filled room groggily for a moment, then glanced down and immediately realized the reason. His hands and feet were both bound tightly with ropes!

His head was pounding from whatever had been in the "tea" that Zeus had given him. Looking around, he saw that the others were still unconscious and also bound like he was.

Crumb betrayed us! The thought ran over and over in his mind as he tried to nudge Abigail awake with his shoulder, something difficult to do with his limited mobility.

"Abigail . . . Abigail!" Andy whispered hoarsely, trying to keep his voice low in case Zeus was nearby. "Wake up!"

When she didn't move, Andy nudged her harder. "Wake up!" he hissed.

"Huhhnnnh . . ." Abigail groaned.

"Wake up, Abigail! We've been captured!"

The girl's long eyelashes flickered and she raised her head slowly from the cushion she'd been using as a pillow.

"What?" she began. And then, seeing that she was bound, like Andy, she snapped into focus.

"It was a trick!" she exclaimed.

"Shhh," said Andy. "Not so loud. Zeus might be nearby."

The two set about waking the others the best they

could, worming their way across the benches and cabin floor to the sides of their comrades. After several difficult minutes, the entire group was alert and ready to make plans to escape the situation.

"Good thing Zeus doesn't know about my hook's abilities," said Rusty. "If someone can help me twist the activation knob, I can change it from hook mode to a knife. We'll be out of here before you can say 'warthog whiskers.'"

Andy edged himself over so that he was back-to-back with the bush pilot.

"I can't reach it!" Andy whispered as he strained. "The angle is all wrong."

"Keep trying," encouraged Rusty. "Remember, a J.E.S. member never gives up."

Easy for you to say, Andy thought as he continued stretching his fingers toward the switch on the side of Rusty's hook. *You're not the one trying to do this.*

It took some doing, but eventually Andy just managed to get his fingers around the switch and turn it.

After a couple of attempts where the hook changed to a crowbar, a telescope, and a lighter, he finally managed to get it to knife mode.

"Well done!" encouraged Betty and Dotty in unison.

A clumping noise above their heads froze them into silence. Someone was walking above decks and headed toward the cabin.

"Quick, back to your places, everybody!" hissed Abigail.

Everyone quickly obeyed, and Rusty made sure that he was lying in such a way that his Swiss Army hook was carefully hidden.

The thumping grew louder. Then there was a loud creak of hinges as the hatch was thrown open and someone descended the stairs with a heavy, limping gait.

Nicodemus Crumb grinned at his bound captives, exposing his crooked yellow teeth. When he got to Andy, the boy watched, horrified, as the old man reached into his pocket and pulled out Andy's ring of J.E.S. keys.

"The Potentate will pay me well for these," he said, examining them closely. "You really shouldn't have told me that Andy is the Jungle Explorers' Society Keymaster, Mr. Bucketts," Crumb added with a glance at the bush pilot. "That was a mistake on your part."

"The only mistake I made was trusting you," growled Rusty. "How long have you been a traitor, Crumb?"

"Not a traitor. I'm not on any side. I'm simply a businessman. Always have been and always will be." He walked over, leaned close to Rusty, and said in a low voice, "Lostmore is too trusting. That's how he got his head shrunk. You'd do well to remember that." He punctuated the last word with sharp clack of his yellowed teeth.

Zeus came down the stairs behind Crumb, his long shadow filling the cabin. "The sails are set, Captain," he said. "We should arrive at the Forbidden Islands by nightfall."

Andy glared at Crumb. "The Forbidden Islands? Where's that? You lied to us—you said you were taking us to the start of the path that leads to the Eternal Tree."

"I never lie," said Crumb pointedly. "But I also don't always reveal all of the truth. The Forbidden Islands are just off the coast of South America. Mostly jungle, pretty much an extension of the Amazon forest. It is where the legends say the Eternal Tree exists, and that is where I will take you. However, after that, I'll be moving on, selling those keys of yours to the Potentate for a pretty penny. As I said before, my shop hasn't been making much money lately."

Andy felt waves of impotent rage wash over him as Crumb and Zeus exited the cabin and closed the hatch behind them. He wondered if the jujus that Zeus had distributed to the group were truly magical items. If so, why had he decided to help them?

There's more to this whole situation than meets the eye, Andy thought. *Maybe Zeus is on our side but is working as a spy.*

On Andy's last adventure, he'd been fooled by the Potentate's use of the Golden Paw, a talisman capable of transforming the appearance of its user into almost any form imaginable. Could it be possible that Zeus was keeping an eye on Crumb? And if so, did Ned know what was going on?

Trying to figure such things out only made his headache worse. He glanced over at Rusty and saw, to his immense relief, that as soon as their captors had left the cabin, he'd commenced cutting the ropes that bound his wrists with his knife attachment. Andy suppressed an urge to cheer when he saw Rusty's arms pop free of their bonds and the ropes fall away from his gleaming appendage.

"Now, for the rest of you lot," said Rusty with a fierce grin.

After everyone had been cut loose, they gathered in a close huddle. Andy rubbed at the raw welts on his wrist as he leaned in close with the others, formulating a plan for what they should do next.

"There's six of us and only two of them," said Rusty. "How hard could it be?"

"That giant might give us a bit of a problem," muttered Abigail.

"I'm not so sure," whispered Andy. "I think he might be secretly on our side."

Rusty's eyes narrowed. "How do you figure? Just because he gave us a bunch of useless trinkets doesn't mean he's with us. It was just a ruse to keep us occupied while he drugged us."

Andy and Abigail exchanged glances. He had to admit Rusty had a point. Andy shrugged and motioned for the bush pilot to continue.

Rusty nodded at Andy, then gazed at the others in the huddled group. "Now then, we're going to take over the ship. Ladies and gentleman, it's time for a good old-fashioned mutiny."

Chapter Eight
Mutiny

For Andy, the hardest part about the plan to take the ship from Crumb and Zeus was the waiting. It seemed like hours since they'd taken their positions in the cabin, waiting for Crumb to return. Everyone was armed with whatever they could lay their hands on to defend themselves, since Crumb had made sure to remove all their regular weapons.

Fortunately, the old man hadn't known about Andy's Zoomwriter, which looked like an ordinary fountain pen.

The boy was glad to have it safely in his front pocket. He would use it if needed. But for now, he was armed with a boat hook, and he held it at the ready as he stared intently at the locked hatch, waiting for their captors to return.

The cabin was stuffy and the sweat stung his eyes as it dripped off his forehead. Andy tried to keep his adrenaline in check as he gripped his makeshift weapon.

Finally, after what felt like forever, they heard the footsteps of their captors approaching the hatch.

But when the hatch opened, things didn't go precisely as planned.

Because he was feeling anxious, Andy lunged too soon. Instead of tripping Crumb and Zeus as they descended the stairs as he was supposed to, he ended up tripping on the boat hook himself, sprawling headlong along the stairs that led into the cabin!

Rusty, seeing that the ambush attempt was threatened, responded immediately, shouting, "Charge!"

And from that moment on, everything was chaos.

Fists flew and kicks landed on both friend and foe, and for a long moment, in spite of the difference in numbers, it wasn't apparent which side was going to win. The tangle of bodies on the floor of the cabin writhed and shouted, cursed and fought until finally, with a last, mighty blow from Betty and Dotty to the jaw of Nicodemus Crumb, it ended.

The entire group of Jungle Explorers was scratched, bruised, and exhausted. With some effort, they managed to tie up Crumb and Zeus, then stood over them, breathing hard.

Andy mumbled, "Sorry." But everyone was too preoccupied to listen. Then he quickly retrieved his keys from the glowering, bruised Crumb and put them safely back into his pocket.

"Betty, Dotty, see if you can locate any navigation maps. We need to figure out where we are and where these Forbidden Islands are," said Rusty. "Abigail, I assume you know about boats from your father. Can you get control of the ship?"

"Absolutely," she said, then dashed up the stairs.

"We're practically there already," growled Crumb. "This is idiotic. I told you I would drop you off there, and I always keep my word."

Rusty lowered his big face to Crumb's and said in a dangerous tone, "So you say. But you stole Andy's keys, and that alone is enough reason not to trust you." He wheeled back to Betty and Dotty and barked, "Let's go, ladies!"

"On it," the sisters said in unison, and left to search the captain's quarters.

Andy then found himself alone with Rusty, Zeus, and Crumb. Rusty stood over their bound captives, the point of his knife hovering threateningly over their throats. Crumb stared back at him with a baleful expression, bruised and swollen from the skirmish.

"Ned trusted you," spat Rusty. "I can't believe you betrayed us like this, Nicodemus."

Crumb leered at the bush pilot. "A man has to make a living, Bucketts. Besides, your esteemed 'leader' has no chance now that the Potentate has the Doomsday Device. I told you—once it's activated, there's no way to stop it. You're all doomed!"

He began to cackle, which only increased Rusty's ire. But Andy's attention was on Zeus. He noticed that the giant didn't have the same attitude as Crumb. The big man didn't look as if he cared whether or not he was captured, but instead sat quietly and serenely stared down at his huge-knuckled hands.

Rusty looked like he was about to deliver a powerful right hook to Crumb's nose, but then he seemed to think better of it. Turning to Andy, he said, "Keep an eye on these two. If either of them makes an attempt at escaping, shout. I'm going to find our weapons and supplies."

And with that, the bush pilot stomped up the stairs and onto the deck with the others.

Andy turned back to Zeus. He wanted to ask him if he really was on their side, and whether the jujus he'd given them would actually help.

But he never got the chance. Just as Andy opened his mouth to speak, a terrific *CRUNCH!* rattled through the hull of the ship. Shouts were heard above decks as Andy was thrown off his feet and sent crashing to the teak floor. The next thing he knew, turbulent seawater was flooding the cabin.

Andy splashed toward the hatch, the water quickly rising to his ankles. He raced above decks and saw the panicked expressions of his friends, all rushing to the port side of the ship to see what they had struck.

"We hit a reef!" Rusty shouted, then wheeled on Betty and Dotty, who were next to Abigail at the ship's wheel. "I thought I told you to consult the maps!"

"We did!" Betty snapped back. "The reef wasn't on the charts!"

Andy gazed toward the horizon, where he could make out the hazy outline of a shoreline.

"There's land over there," he said to Rusty. "If Crumb wasn't lying, then I guess those are the Forbidden Islands. But we might have to swim for it. There's water filling the cabin below. . . . I . . . I . . . don't think we have very long, and I didn't see any lifeboats when we boarded the ship. . . ."

His voice trailed off. He'd suddenly remembered that Nicodemus Crumb and Zeus were tied up in the cabin with the water rising. In spite of the fact that they were enemies, Andy couldn't let them die.

"Crumb and Zeus!" he said by way of explanation as he turned and dashed toward the hatch that led below.

"Let 'em fend for themselves!" shouted Rusty. "They betrayed us!"

Andy turned back to Rusty, his expression serious. "They don't deserve to die. That's not what we do in the J.E.S. We're better than that."

Rusty started to protest, but Andy turned back and ran toward the hatchway.

When he got below, he saw that the water was rising fast. But then, to his surprise, he also saw that the ropes that had bound the two men had been cut and were now floating on top of the water. The jagged hole that had ripped the side of the ship had been opened even more, probably kicked to pieces by the two men, and they had apparently escaped and made a swim for safety.

With the water now up to his knees, Andy waded up the stairway and back above decks. He scanned the horizon, shielding his eyes with his hand, but there was no sign of either Crumb or Zeus as far as he could see.

But he didn't have time to consider the matter further, for at that moment the broken hull of the Chinese junk lurched suddenly as the vessel sank deeper into the sea, sending Andy and the rest of the crew flying out into the dark water.

A large beam crashed into Andy as he fell, the impact shoving him down, down, down into the depths of the sea. As the water closed around him, he was dimly aware of other shapes in the waves, but whether they were sharks or people he couldn't tell.

Andy clung to the beam with both arms, knowing that it was his best and only chance to survive and hoping against hope that the wood would float and that somehow his friends were okay.

The Potentate stood on a rocky outcropping high above the ocean. Her black hair whipped in the wind behind her like a pirate's flag, and her face was covered by an expressionless ivory mask. She wore her traveling clothes, all black, and the effect was intimidating. Her appearance was certain to strike fear in the hearts of anyone who saw her.

And that, of course, was what she wanted above all else.

"Bring me the device," she ordered.

A servant with a twisted back hobbled up next to her. He was as old and gnarled as a twisted oak tree. As he handed her the large carved clock, he said in a whiny, high-pitched voice, "Is it time, Mistress?"

She didn't reply. After taking the Doomsday Device from his twisted grip, she set it down on a flat stone.

"Snapjaw!" She turned on her crumpled assistant.

"Yes, Mistress?"

"Bring the others," she commanded.

"I hear and obey, Mistress," Snapjaw said as he hobbled off.

The Potentate removed the scrap of parchment from the Library of Alexandria from a hidden pocket in her cloak. Behind her mask, she smiled as she gazed down at the single phrase written there in ancient Greek. She'd given up much to implement her plan, and many of her followers' lives had been spent in getting her to this moment in time.

Time, she mused as she stared down at the horrible carvings on the clock. She was older than most people knew and had seen a lot of it.

But of all the time she'd lived, the next twelve hours would be the most torturous for her enemies—and the most fulfilling for her personally. Soon, she would have the entire arsenal of the Jungle Explorers' Society's artifacts at her disposal, and her legions of criminal soldiers would be unstoppable.

She traced the first carving on the clock with her long-nailed finger. The bloodred nail traced the outline of a figure with its mouth wide open with terror. The Potentate had studied many dark manuscripts to find out exactly how the Doomsday Device worked. Every hour, she would visit new tortures upon her victims until they bent to her will. None would be able to withstand twelve hours of the torment she would inflict. In the end, even the great Ned Lostmore would prefer to give her what she wanted rather than endure the horrors that were in store for him and his followers.

The steady thud of several booted feet announced Snapjaw's return. He was surrounded by ten of her most trusted members of the Collective, all of whom were the most dangerous cutthroats and master criminals ever known.

They had served her well.

She indicated the carvings on the clock with a wave of her hand. Even the most hardened of the criminals who worked with her looked nervous.

"Wind the clock."

Snapjaw obeyed immediately, cranking the large stone winding key that was embedded in the side of the device. Once it was wound, the clock awaited the final command, the secret words of death that had to be spoken in order to activate it.

Beneath her mask, the Potentate's lips were stretched in a feline grin. Hunger was in her eyes, like a tigress about to inflict torture upon her prey. When she spoke, her voice rang out in a guttural growl.

"Chronos Thánatos!"

And the magic words, which had never been spoken before, caused the second hand on the Doomsday Device to begin its fateful tick. . . .

Chapter Nine
Carnivorous Vines

Andy woke from unconsciousness with ocean water swirling around his toes. The broken beam that had saved his life was nearby, but aside from that familiar object, he could see nothing else on the beach.

He coughed, expelling seawater from his lungs.

Andy had just shakily risen to his knees when a deafening noise rang through the air. It was so loud that it sent the treetops trembling as if they'd been buffeted by a strong wind, and Andy staggered and retched again—not from the seawater this time, but from the sudden feeling of nausea that had come from nowhere.

The sound wasn't thunder.

It was a single chime.

It was the same sound a clock makes when striking the time, only much, much louder.

And Andy knew, with a terrible feeling in the pit of his stomach, what it was. His instinct was confirmed when a second later there was a high-pitched whine, a whistle of such high frequency that it felt like his head would explode.

And then, worst of all, a feminine voice . . . low and commanding, it seemed to speak directly inside his head.

Attention, Jungle Explorers' Society! Give me the location of your hidden artifacts and you will be spared torments that you cannot imagine. For every hour that you resist, you will be subjected to pain such as you've never felt before. All I ask is that you speak the words I hear and obey, and you will immediately join the ranks of the Collective. All discomfort will cease. This is your only warning. . . .

And then the voice in Andy's head went silent, as did the painful ringing. His hands were white and they trembled. He was sure that if he were to look in a mirror, his face would look very much like the first one carved into the Doomsday Device . . . a face filled with fear.

But in spite of the fear he felt, Andy didn't speak the words that the Potentate had told him to.

Never that!

But even as he resisted her command to speak his obedience to her, he worried about the painful tortures that would be sure to come next. If all that had happened so far was the terrible ringing in his ears, just how bad would the other things be?

"Well, at least I have an hour before the first plague comes," he said, trying to comfort himself. He gazed again at the overgrown path in front of him and then glanced back out over the ocean behind him. There was no sign of the Chinese junk anywhere . . . just a flat line of ocean.

He was alone.

And although he was soaked to the skin and feeling weak, he decided that he'd best go forward, because there wasn't any time to lose.

The Doomsday Device had been activated.

And he had to find out what had happened to the others.

After crossing the threshold of overhanging branches, Andy discovered that everything growing around him was so thick that it nearly blocked out all sunlight.

There could be all kinds of man-eating snakes and who knows what else in here, he thought.

As he fought his way forward down the path, brushing elephant ear leaves aside, he wondered if the path he was on was anywhere near the tree they sought. Had Crumb been telling the truth about this being where the tree was supposed to be located? The odds didn't seem good. After all, Crumb had stolen his keys and planned to sell them to their enemies.

After a very sweaty twenty minutes of tearing through

the brush with his bare hands, Andy was relieved to find that he'd emerged into a clearing.

While catching his breath, Andy noticed an unusual type of tree at the edge of the clearing. It seemed to be nothing more than a tangle of roots and vines.

I wonder....

Feeling curious, Andy cautiously moved toward it. It didn't look like a legendary tree that had been around since the beginning of time. But it did look unlike any tree he'd ever seen. He was surprised to see fruit growing among the tree's roots.

Oranges? he thought. *Growing by the roots? How strange!*

The roots and vines seemed to be the bottom of an orange tree, with the majority of what would normally have been the branches submerged below the earth; only a few poked out, allowing the anemic oranges to ripen. Overall, the effect was uncanny. It just didn't make sense that the familiar tree was growing upside down.

It made Andy feel ill at ease. What was this place?

It certainly was like no jungle that he'd ever been in so far. The plants were varied and different, with an assortment of species he'd never encountered during his time with the J.E.S. *So strange*, Andy mused.

A sudden high-pitched scream nearly startled him out of his boots. Andy whipped around and saw, to his dismay, that he recognized the person who had screamed—and could see in an instant why she'd done so!

Abigail Awol was wrapped in vines that writhed around her arms, torso, and neck as if they were hungry pythons.

A carnivorous plant!

"Hang on, Abigail! I'm coming!" shouted Andy. He reached for his Zoomwriter as he ran, filled with a mixture of fear and relief at seeing his friend. Abigail was fighting like a trapped animal, clawing and biting at the relentless vines, but for every one that she injured, a new one seemed to take its place.

Andy scanned the base of the plant, looking for a

vulnerable spot. Seeing a patch of trunk that was unprotected, he uncapped his Zoomwriter and activated the atomic pulse emitter.

BOOOOOM!

The shock wave that left the fountain pen sounded like a thunderclap. The plant, having never met such powerful resistance, immediately loosened its hold on Abigail and emitted a prolonged screech of pain from somewhere in its inhuman mass.

As soon as Abigail dropped to the ground, she scuttled backward, crab-like, as fast as she could away from the terrifying plant.

Breathing hard, she turned to Andy and gave him a fierce embrace. "I thought I was alone and everyone was dead!" she said.

Andy hugged her back and chuckled mirthlessly. "Well, I'm not. At least not yet," he added with a rueful grin. "Between that horrible thing and the plagues that are coming, I'm grateful for every minute I'm still breathing."

"Did you hear the chime?" Abigail asked.

Andy nodded.

"It was horrible," she said and suppressed a shudder.

"I know," said Andy.

Abigail wiped her sweaty forehead. "Have you seen any of the others since the shipwreck?"

Andy shook his head. "When I woke up I was alone."

"Venomade," said Abigail.

"What?" asked Andy.

"The drink Zeus gave us. I've been thinking about it ever since and finally recognized it. It's a potion my father taught me to make, often used by witch doctors to subdue their patients. Powerful stuff."

"I'll say," replied Andy.

It felt good to talk after being so anxious and alone.

"Can you walk okay?" Andy asked, helping Abigail to her feet.

She stood, a little wobbly at first. "I'm fine," she replied. "But I wouldn't be if you hadn't come along when you did. Thanks for saving me back there."

"You've rescued *me* more times than I can count," said Andy. "Come on . . . as much as I don't want to, we'd better keep moving. The sooner we can find Patrick Begorra, the better!"

Chapter Ten
Birds and Beasts

Both Andy and Abigail were caught off guard when the second chime of the Doomsday Device rang. They had been walking for about an hour and had discovered a stream. When the chime sounded, they were following the trickle of fetid black water deeper into the forest. The air was thick with mosquitoes, and their incessant buzzing and biting had been so distracting that Andy had momentarily lost track of time.

But he was jolted back into reality by the thunderous peal of the clock. It struck two times before echoing into silence.

Andy and Abigail exchanged worried glances. Once again, the painful, high-pitched noise filled their ears as the Potentate, her voice magically transmitted via the dark artifact, echoed in their minds.

Give me the artifacts or bear the consequences.

The voice abruptly faded along with the terrible noise. Andy looked over at Abigail and saw that she, like himself, had been holding her hands over her ears. But because the voice was magically transmitted inside their heads, it hadn't made a bit of difference; it was simply a reflexive action.

Then the pain came.

The first of the Doomsday Device's curses was a searing, white-hot pain that started behind the eyes and then spread to all their extremities. Andy and Abigail screamed and fell to their knees. It felt like fire was shooting through every nerve, and Andy realized that he'd never truly felt pain before that moment.

And as if that weren't bad enough, it turned out that it was those very screams that attracted the predators.

As soon as the first jolt of pain faded and Andy gasped for breath, he heard a loud rustling from somewhere behind him. Still shaking from the terrible clock's torture, he turned and saw the biggest Bengal tiger he'd ever seen emerge from behind a large fern. It plodded toward them, its eyes an unnaturally burning crimson. To Andy, who had encountered several evil things summoned by cursed artifacts during his J.E.S. adventures, it seemed that the creature must have been created from dark magic.

The air practically crackled with evil energy.

"C-careful," said Abigail in a shaky voice. "It looks hungry."

"Let's back up slowly," said Andy weakly. "Don't stare at it directly. Cats take that as a challenge."

Not really knowing what else to do, they stepped slowly backward, trying as hard as they could to not let their anxiety show. The gigantic animal let out a low, threatening growl.

"Get your pen," said Abigail.

"It needs to recharge. It's not ready."

"We have to do something!"

Andy felt a sinking feeling in his chest. The situation looked dire. But then, just as things looked as if they couldn't get any worse, a great clamor arose from the trees. Glancing upward, Andy immediately wished he hadn't.

Dozens of gigantic apes with the same glowing red eyes leapt from the branches. Their fangs were bared and they roared a challenge as they dropped to the ground. The earth shook where they landed, and Andy and Abigail instantly knew that they were surrounded.

So this is how we'll die, thought Andy. *Not by the Doomsday Device, but at the hands of vicious animals the size of which I'd never imagined possible!*

The circle around them began to close. Andy's heart nearly thudded out of his chest. *What do I do? What do I do?*

But it was Abigail who did something. A high note split the air, not a terrible, painful sound, but something light and wonderfully sweet. The animals stopped their advance with puzzled expressions. Andy glanced over and saw that Abigail had the birdcall juju—the parrot-shaped necklace charm that Zeus had given her—next to her ruby lips, raised high as she blew it like a whistle.

Now we'll find out whether it really works or not, thought Andy.

He didn't have to wait long. Suddenly, the air around them filled with the sound of flapping wings. Then there were voices, uniquely parroty voices, calling among them.

"There they are, lads!" said one in an Irish accent.

"Here, kitty, kitty!" said another in a German accent. "Nice kitty!"

And then, flocks and flocks of multicolored tropical birds streaked from the sky, carrying tiny objects carved in the shape of pineapples in their talons.

Andy felt his heart leap with recognition.

"They're from the Tiki Room!" he said excitedly. "Madame Wiki must have sent them! How did they find us . . . ?"

He didn't have a chance to finish his sentence. Soon, the ground all around them was exploding wherever the parrots dropped their pineapple-shaped cargo, the tiny artifacts detonating on impact against the soft terrain.

Even though the apes and tiger were magically summoned creatures, the concussive explosions knocked them back on their haunches and sent them screaming back into the jungle.

Andy and Abigail were thrown off their feet as well, but recovered quickly as the birds flew down to roost in the trees all around them.

One particular bird, a white cockatiel, flew directly over to Andy and landed on his shoulder.

"Hoku!" Andy said, surprised. "Am I glad to see you!"

The bird, one Andy had met during his first adventure, nuzzled Andy's cheek affectionately.

"Andy needed help and Hoku came, she did. Hoku

came when Andy needed help. Hoku heard the call, the special call, and Madame Wiki gave us weapons for helping, yes, she did!" The bird prattled on in her excited singsong voice. Then she spotted the birdcall juju hanging around Abigail's neck.

"Abigail's juju? Not Andy's? Abigail's, not Andy's?" she asked, sounding puzzled.

Abigail grinned at her. "Yes, and I had no idea what it would do," she confessed. She glanced down at the carved pendant with affection mixed with a little sadness. "I only wish it had more than one use."

"*Oui!*" said Pierre, a beautifully plumed parrot. "Eet eez very special—mageek! Where did you get eet?"

"From Zeus," replied Andy.

"Hoku knows Zeus, Hoku knows Zeus!" the bird chirped happily. "Zeus is brother to Madame Wiki. Zeus knows many things!"

Andy's question was finally answered. His instincts had been right . . . Zeus had been on their side after all. He suddenly wondered if he'd been able to swim to safety, and if so, would he be able to make his way to Madame Wiki?

If it hadn't been for the juju, they would most certainly have been eaten or worse by now. Andy wished he could thank the giant for helping them.

"Please tell Madame Wiki thank you for us," said Andy. "You saved our lives!"

"Hoku will!"

She nuzzled Andy's cheek with her beak. Then, with a great rushing of wings, all the birds took off back into the air. Andy couldn't help calling after them, shouting, "Stay! We could use your help!"

But even as he shouted, he knew it was no good. Zeus's words came back to him, echoing in his thoughts.

One use!

Except unlike when he'd spoken them before, in context the words made sense.

Chapter Eleven
Rusty

Andy and Abigail set off down the trail immediately, following the winding black creek deeper into the jungle. It was the closest thing to a path that either of them could see. They were both still weak from the last attack of the Doomsday Device, but Andy could feel that he was growing steadily stronger as time ticked by.

At least until the next chime, he thought anxiously.

He tried to remember what he could from his scouting manual about reading the time from the position of the sun. Unfortunately, the trees were so thick that only a little weak sunlight leaked in from time to time. On the few occasions when it did, Andy glanced skyward and tried to estimate how much time they had until the next strike of the clock, but he really couldn't tell.

Under the circumstances, it was impossible not to feel completely on edge.

But fortunately, for the next several minutes, they didn't run into any more magically summoned animals. Once, they heard a loud rustle off in the distance and quickened their pace in response to it, moving as fast as they could while trying not to make a sound.

The stream, which had been barely a trickle, eventually grew into a sluggish river. Andy and Abigail paused to look at the murky water and catch their breath.

"I don't know about you, but I'm starving," said Andy.

"I was just thinking that, too," said Abigail. "Unfortunately for us, all our supplies went down with the ship."

Andy glanced around. "I wonder if there's any fruit? There's no shortage of trees around here."

"Yeah, did you notice how many different kinds there are?" said Abigail, brightening. "It's uncanny!"

She pointed at a large-leafed plant nearby. "*Cyperus alternifolius*. An umbrella plant. And there's a *Syagrus romanzoffiana*, commonly known as a queen palm. Oh! And there's a *Distictis buccinatoria* . . . a Mexican blood flower!"

"Mexico? Seems like this jungle has plants from all over the place. Why are they all here?"

Abigail shrugged. "Beats me. I still have no idea where we are. I've never seen a jungle like this on any map, and believe me, my father made me study my fair share of them." She brushed a stray hair from her forehead.

Andy was about to start looking for fruit when an earsplitting cry sounded from across the riverbank. Andy and Abigail wheeled around in time to see a big man, tattered and bloody, come hurtling out of the jungle and plunge into the river.

"Rusty!" they both shouted in alarm, recognizing the bush pilot. The pilot spotted them, and with eyes wide as wagon wheels, he screamed two words as he swam toward them.

"Run! Dingonek!"

To anyone else, the word *Dingonek* wouldn't have made much sense. But Andy remembered the terrible legendary creature they'd encountered before, a horrible crocodile-like thing that had been summoned with a dark magic artifact and had teeth like razors.

And it had taken Rusty's hand with a single bite!

At the time, Andy had believed that it was the only one, a single creature from myth and legend. But when he saw the thing following close behind Rusty Bucketts, twice as big as he remembered, he didn't take time to wonder how it had gotten there.

He ran. And so did Abigail.

Rusty splashed and spluttered to shore and quickly caught up with them, propelled by the horror of his worst nightmare. The Dingonek had taken one body part, and he certainly didn't want it to take anything else!

The leaves and branches slapped at Andy's face

and arms, drawing deep scratches and cuts, but he paid them no heed. He ran like hell itself was on his heels, and even still, he could hear the loud crashing behind the three of them getting louder.

"It's ... gaining ... on ... us!" Abigail shouted between breaths.

What am I doing? Andy suddenly thought. He wheeled around, stopping dead in his tracks. Abigail shot him a panicked glance.

"Andy!"

But he'd suddenly come to his senses. He didn't need to run . . . he could fight back! He whipped his Zoomwriter from his pocket and aimed at the huge prehistoric-looking amphibious lizard that crashed through the bushes behind them. When it saw him, the Dingonek let out a ferocious roar.

BOOOOM!

The pen had had time to recharge, and the blast from the barrel did its work. The Dingonek hurtled backward almost fifty yards. The others stopped running and turned to watch as the great beast landed with a splash back in the river.

"That . . . won't keep him for long," huffed Rusty. Andy glanced at him, glad to see him but also alarmed at how beat up and pale he looked.

"What happened to you?" asked Abigail.

"Wandered into the jungle after the shipwreck," said Rusty, looking around anxiously. "For now, we need to get the Dingonek off our scent. Follow me."

He plunged through the jungle. Andy and Abigail had no choice but to follow. Rusty took them in a wide half circle, twisting and turning through various spots difficult for a creature the size of the Dingonek to traverse, then crossed the river farther downstream to ensure that the monster wouldn't be able to track them by scent.

They were dripping wet. And although Abigail and Andy didn't have nearly as many cuts and bruises as Rusty, they both felt like they'd been run over by a convoy of trucks.

"Any sign of Betty and Dotty?" asked Andy.

"How should I know?" spluttered Rusty. "All I know is that after being washed up like a drowned rat and entering this blasted jungle, I'm fairly certain that this is the most dangerous mission I've ever attempted. I've been nearly killed ten times already."

And just then, before Andy or Abigail could reply, the sound they'd come to dread echoed through the air. The third chime of the Doomsday Device struck, and with it, the same painful ringing in their ears.

Swear your allegiance to me and give me the artifacts. Obey me and stand by my side....

Andy, Abigail, and Rusty exchanged worried glances. Each could tell what the other was thinking. *There's no way I'll ever swear allegiance to her*, thought Andy. But on the heels of that thought was *I wonder what's coming next?*

Unfortunately, none of them had to wait long to find out.

Chapter Twelve
Betty and Dotty

The boils that sprouted on their arms, legs, and backs were painful. But what made them infinitely worse was the fact that they itched like crazy. And with every scratch, burning pain seared from the wound, causing the three explorers to gasp and curse with every attempt to relieve their discomfort.

Rusty roared like an angry bear. "Blast the Potentate and all she stands for!" he shouted.

"Keep it down," said Abigail. "You might attract more of those giant animals."

Andy was so uncomfortable he forgot that he was hungry. Every movement he made seemed to irritate the red bumps. It was torture!

"Let's just keep moving," he said. "The sooner we find Patrick Begorra, the sooner this will all be over."

"You mean *if* we find him," Rusty grumbled. Then he added, "Remember, Crumb thought the tree was somewhere on this island, and he never found it. We don't even know for sure if we're on the right path! Besides, if we do find him, then what?" He grimaced as he scratched one of his festering boils. He didn't have to finish the statement for Andy and Abigail to know what he'd been about to say. It was a harsh reminder that even if they found the leprechaun, there was no certainty that he would be willing and able to help them stop the Doomsday Device.

But what other chance have we got? thought Andy. He knew that Rusty must really be feeling miserable, because his usual optimism wasn't there.

Feeling downtrodden, the three set off down the winding path by the river once more. Fortunately, it had grown a bit wider than when Andy and Abigail first found it and was easier to follow.

The mosquitoes were still thick and the air humid. The trees, which had been varied before, became more uniform.

Eucalyptus, Andy observed. The tall trees gave off a pleasant scent, the only refreshing thing that they had experienced in a while, and Andy was grateful for it. "Abigail said that the 'tea' Zeus gave us was actually venomade," Andy said to Rusty, trying to make conversation.

"Figures," said Rusty. "I've heard of it, of course. Your grandfather said that during his encounter with Bungalow Bob, the witch doctor, he was forced to drink it."

"Wait," said Andy. "You mean the witch doctor at that hidden temple, the one who shrank his head?"

"The same," Rusty grunted with a nod. "That's why

he can't recall everything that happened. When he woke up, he was in the . . . er . . . condition he's in now."

Andy had a queasy feeling when he thought about his grandfather's encounter. In all his adventures to date, there hadn't been much that frightened him more than the idea that such a thing was possible. He couldn't imagine a worse fate than having his head shrunk and then being imprisoned in a glass cabinet for the rest of his life.

Grandfather always said to be careful around jungle magic, Andy thought.

He scratched the bumps on his arm, wincing. He thought about his parents. They thought he was spending a rather uneventful summer at his grandfather's mansion. He realized that he missed them. He wanted to go home, tell them about the adventures he'd had, and show them how much he'd learned.

For the first time since he'd started going on adventures, he felt a wave of homesickness. He missed his mother's home cooking, especially her fried chicken and mashed potatoes. He also missed the quiet evenings playing chess with his father, when they talked about their days and he told Andy about the latest books he'd acquired at the town library. His father had been the librarian in Thousand Oaks for the last thirty years and knew every single book on the shelf. Andy's eyes stung a little and he wiped them quickly before the others could see.

If we can just get to the tree and end all this, I'll never take them for granted again.

A sudden movement in the foliage on his left startled him. But before he could react, one of the terrible vines that had trapped Abigail snaked out and grabbed his ankle.

"Help!" shouted Andy as he was dragged rapidly backward, bumping and banging over the rocks and foliage toward the hungry man-eating plant. He struggled, kicking his trapped leg as hard as he could, but he couldn't wrest himself free. Before Abigail or Rusty had time to respond, a battle cry emerged from the

bushes and a figure came flying through the air.

Two figures, actually.

Betty and Dotty were masters of the martial arts, and with a well-aimed slice, they cut through the vine in a single swipe of their deadly knives as they flew past Andy and landed in an expert crouch on the other side.

The plant let out a horrible screech as sap spewed from the opened wound. Betty and Dotty grabbed Andy by the back of his shirt and, with one strong jerk, hoisted him to his feet.

"Run!" Betty bellowed, and Andy didn't have to be told twice. Together, he and the twins dashed back to the river, where a stunned Rusty and Abigail stood, staring.

"Go, go, go! There's something much worse than those vines behind us, and that's saying a lot!" shouted Dotty.

Galvanized into action, the five of them raced downriver, staying as close as possible to the banks without losing sight of the parallel path they'd been following.

While they ran, they heard an unearthly howl from somewhere behind them. Andy couldn't stop images of werewolves and other monsters from entering his mind as he ran. He had no idea what was back there, but from the look of panic on the normally serene sisters' faces, he knew it had to be something terrible.

They were so busy running and looking back over their shoulders for any sign of pursuit that they failed to notice the pile of dead branches on the path. To the observant eye, the placement of the branches was incongruous with the rest of the terrain. They were haphazardly organized into a kind of lattice that covered a hole.

Which everyone discovered as they tumbled down into the darkness.

Andy didn't even have time to scream before they hit the bottom, falling together in a painful heap. He landed on his side with the wind knocked out of him, unable to breathe.

Then everything went black.

Andy must have been unconscious for almost an hour, because it was the chime of the Doomsday Device that woke him up, echoing in the cavern that they'd fallen into with redoubled volume and sending a paralyzing feeling of dread through the entire group.

He opened his eyes, feeling dizzy.

Then the voice that had become all too familiar echoed in each of their heads along with the persistent ringing noise. And this time, Andy noticed that the Potentate didn't have a long speech. She said only four words. But they were the four words that, when acted upon, would stop the torment. For the first time, Andy wondered if listening to them and doing what they said might be better than the misery he'd been enduring— and the unknown misery that was yet to come. All he had to do was reach into his pocket and offer her the keys. . . .

Give me the artifacts.

Chapter Thirteen
The Potentate's Army

Her heart swelled with pride as she surveyed her army.

The Collective.

They all awaited her orders . . . and she, a new dark empress of unlimited power, was ready to tell them her commands. Once she had the J.E.S. and their artifacts under her control, together they would be able to conquer the entire world.

The idea felt very good. And the Potentate seemed to swell with the sense of power that the Doomsday Device had afforded her.

There was only one thing that troubled her, and it was the fact that none of the Jungle Explorers' Society, her archenemies, had caved in.

Give it time, she told herself. But she was by nature an impulsive person. She wanted what she wanted, and she wanted it *now*. It rankled to be forced to wait, and it put her in a foul temper.

"Your Majesty," came a voice by her shoulder. She turned her blank ivory mask to see who had addressed her. It was one of her loyal soldiers, a woman known as the Velvet Knife. She was an unmatched assassin and had been responsible for the deaths of many unsuspecting world leaders.

"Yes?" the Potentate replied.

"When do we attack?"

The Potentate flicked her wrist in irritation. "Soon."

The Velvet Knife stared up at her with a questioning look. She didn't dare ask what the Potentate was thinking, but her eyes said enough.

Oftentimes, the Potentate wouldn't deign to dispense her private plans to her underlings. But because the Velvet Knife had served her well in the past, she decided to let her in on a little secret.

"I know what they're doing," she said.

"Your Majesty?" the Velvet Knife replied.

"The J.E.S.," the Potentate answered.

When the Velvet Knife remained quiet, she continued.

"They have only one recourse. The pieces on the chessboard are all but taken and only one move remains. They seek the leprechaun."

The Velvet Knife wisely held her tongue, which made her master willing to continue.

"We will march with our vast army to stop them short. Ned Lostmore might think he still has a chance to defeat me, but he has another thing coming."

The Velvet Knife didn't know anything about leprechauns—what they were, whether they existed, or where one might be located. But time and experience serving the Potentate had taught her to disregard her own feelings on the matter and instead accept whatever her master said without question.

"I hear and obey, Your Majesty," the Velvet Knife replied. "We await your command."

Beneath the ivory mask, the Potentate smiled. "I see great things in your future," she said.

And, fingering the handle of her thirsty blade, the Velvet Knife slipped away to communicate what she'd been told to the other lieutenants.

Chapter Fourteen
The Temple Ruins

Andy realized that the pit they'd fallen into was actually part of an underground tunnel. It was dark, damp, and filled with the ends of wriggling worms hanging from the ceiling. But it wasn't the oppressive atmosphere that gave Andy the willies. It was the persistent, horrible scuttling sound in the earthen tunnel. And every time he looked over his shoulder to see what had made the noise, it seemed as if he were too late and had just missed whatever had been haunting his steps.

"I really don't like this place," said Andy.

"Thanks for stating the obvious," replied Abigail.

"No, seriously, I mean it," said Andy.

Maybe it was because the Doomsday Device was taking its toll on all of them, but Andy thought that the entire group looked haggard, and though there were no mirrors nearby, he was fairly certain that he himself looked the same or worse. The last toll of the bell had the effect of turning the boils into something worse. Every festering sore that had decorated their bodies had become a dark, horrible spot. Andy wasn't sure, but it looked like the descriptions he'd read of the plague in medieval Europe. If so, it was a death sentence without treatment, and he knew that as sure as the Doomsday Device was a clock, time was short.

Andy's head swam with fever. He'd never felt more miserable in his entire life.

Rusty had managed to salvage a small amount of provisions from the ship. It wasn't much. The rations were meager and rather wet, but they were better than nothing, and the group members all tried to keep down what they could. Thankfully, none of them had been seriously hurt in the fall. But Andy knew he would be feeling the bruises for days to come; in addition to his new sickness, his ribs already felt sore.

"Does anybody else hear that scuttling noise?" asked Andy as they rounded another corner in the dank tunnel.

"What scuttling noise?" said Abigail.

"That—right there!" said Andy.

Rusty tilted his head to listen in the direction Andy was pointing and then shook it slowly.

"Can't hear a thing," said the bush pilot. "It's probably all in your head. If I were you, I'd keep my ears peeled for animal growls instead." He gazed ahead, looking concerned. "Could be anything in here."

They walked along in silence for a while longer. Andy could have sworn that he still heard the scuttling of insect legs, but since Rusty hadn't heard it, he wondered if he was imagining it. The truth was, any kind of dark, enclosed space frightened him, and he was starting to feel more anxious than he liked to admit.

After a few more minutes of walking, the tunnel opened up and revealed the crumbling ruin of an ancient temple.

"Wow," said Andy. The ruin was impressive. Gigantic chipped blocks of emerald-green stone had unknown deities etched into their surfaces. Looking closer, Andy saw lizard-headed men and women surrounded by human supplicants.

"Does anybody else get the feeling that whoever this temple was built for was not a very nice person?" he asked. Then Andy noticed that there were huge spiders crawling up and down the uppermost stones, and suddenly he knew the scuttling he'd been hearing hadn't all been in his mind.

Oh, great, he thought. *Giant spiders. I hate spiders.*

"Well, let's hope that whoever it was built for isn't upset that we're trespassing. We've got no choice but to go back or go through, and I'm too tired to go back," said Abigail.

And with that, she strode toward the crumbling entrance of the temple without looking back. The others, who weren't in the mood to debate, followed after.

As soon as they walked underneath the stone archway, Andy felt the familiar prickling on his skin that indicated the presence of jungle magic. But instead of something slight, the feeling was very intense and made him so light-headed and dizzy that he had to lean against a nearby pillar for support.

"Anybody else feel that?" he gasped.

"Who couldn't?" exclaimed Rusty. "Whatever is creating that magical field packs one heck of a wallop." He turned a metal knob on his Swiss Army hook, and a sharp blade emerged from the artificial appendage. "Everybody stay on guard."

Andy took his Zoomwriter from his pocket.

They inched forward into the main part of the temple, moving as quietly as they could.

The walls of the interior of the temple were covered with carvings of tiny skulls. Andy glanced at each one as they passed, wondering why they were so small, but then suddenly stopped short, noticing a freshly made carving.

"Look at this!" he exclaimed.

The others gathered around, looking at where Andy was pointing. The stone looked out of place next to the ancient ones. It was of a smallish size and had been crammed in between two of the larger stones. Carved upon it in a neat, elegant hand were three letters.

JES

"What do you think it means?" asked Andy.

"Only one thing," replied Rusty. "That one of our members has already been to this place. Here, see if you can pull it out from between that crack in the stones."

Andy tugged at the rock, and after a bit of effort it popped loose. Tucked behind it was something small, wrapped in a leather casing. Andy removed the little parcel and after undoing the thong that tied it up, opened it to reveal a message in familiar handwriting on a piece of expensive-looking parchment.

To whom it may concern. I have reason to believe that this is the ancient ruin of Ankor-Ra, a temple that once held great power and significance. There is powerful magic here, and, I believe, a great artifact that generates it. I underestimated everything about this place and the witch doctor who resides here. The things that I have seen in this place, beings that have been created by the darkest of artifact magic, would defy the imagination and will most certainly haunt my nightmares for many years to come.

    I write these, perhaps my last words, in hopes that any member of the Society will find them. My name is Ned Lostmore. The witch doctor in this ruin, a man known as Bungalow Bob, has left me for dead. To anyone who finds this

*MESSAGE, PLEASE SEE to it that my grandson, Andy
Stanley, is notified of my untimely demise and
ushered into the Society as my designated heir.
This is my last will and testament.
Kungaloosh.
Ned Lostmore*

Everyone stared at the note, hardly able to believe what they'd all just read.

"I can hardly believe that my grandfather was here," said Andy. "This must be the temple where . . . you know . . . it happened."

The rest of the group knew what Andy meant when he said *it*: Ned Lostmore's encounter with Bungalow Bob, which had ended with his head shrunk. Ned had always been cryptic with the details of the event. He'd somehow escaped, probably with the help of someone in the Society. But at the time he'd written the note, it was obvious that he'd sustained severe injuries and didn't think he was going to survive.

"Why was he here?" asked Abigail.

"He said it was because he was researching some new kind of medical cure that was present in some exotic moth. At least, that's what I was told," said Andy.

"Hogwash," said Rusty. "There's no way he would have come here and braved these dangers for a bit of medicine. I think he was looking for something else." Rusty shared a meaningful glance with the group.

"Do you think he was looking for Begorra?" asked Abigail.

"What else could it be?" said Betty.

"I agree," added Dotty, glancing at her sister. "And something went terribly wrong down here. Ned nearly died."

Everyone was silent as they thought about the implications. A movement to their left caused everyone to turn at once. What they saw took them by such surprise that everyone stood frozen in place for several moments.

"I am Bungalow Bob," came the sound of an elegant, youthful voice. "And you all have the distinct honor of being my latest acquisitions." It seemed strange coming from a man who looked far older and more wrinkled than any Andy had ever seen. He had snowy white hair down to his shoulders and blazing blue eyes, and he was robed in ceremonial clothing with a large headdress. A necklace made of finger bones decorated his neck, and his gaze flashed with undisguised malice.

The ancient witch doctor looked around the group. "Now then, which of you valuable additions to my collection of shrunken heads would like to go first?"

Chapter Fifteen
Bungalow Bob

Bungalow Bob! The name of the witch doctor conjured up horrific visions in Andy's mind. He already felt sick from the plague, but this was too much. Anxiety washed over him. He couldn't stand the thought of facing the same fate as his grandfather!

Rusty was the first to recover his wits and respond to Bungalow Bob's question. "Just what do you mean, *go first*?" he demanded. "And by the way, I'm not interested in becoming part of *anyone's* collection." As he said this, Andy noticed that he twisted a lever on his Swiss Army hook, and a dangerous-looking pointed spike emerged, replacing the blade that had been there earlier.

The witch doctor gazed at Rusty's attempt at intimidation with an amused expression. Then he noticed Abigail for the first time.

"Abigail Awol!" he said. "What on earth are you doing here?"

Andy turned to Abigail with a shocked expression. Bungalow Bob knew her?

Abigail stepped forward. "Hello, Bob. Since we last met, my situation has, er . . . changed a bit."

Bungalow Bob's smile widened. "I'll say it has! I don't recognize any of your new companions. How's Professor Phink?"

"Quite dead, unfortunately," Abigail replied. "An incident with a ravenous Hawaiian deity."

Bungalow Bob's smile never dimmed. "Ah, well, that's part of the job, isn't it?" He noticed the confused expressions of the group and asked, "Tell me, Abigail, who are your traveling companions?"

Andy's head spun. Bungalow Bob had gone from threatening their lives to suddenly acting like he was receiving guests for a party. Who knew what he would do next?

Abigail introduced each one in turn, keeping her tone even and conversational as if she were trying to prevent another volatile reaction. When she got to Andy, Bob's eyes brightened.

"You don't say!" he exclaimed happily. "The grandson of Ned Lostmore? How wonderful!" Before Andy knew what was happening, Bob had bounded over and was pumping his hand up and down. "Truly a pleasure to meet you. Your grandfather is my greatest competitor!"

Andy stared up at the eccentric fellow, feeling more confused than ever. This was the same person who had shrunk his grandfather's head, and he was acting like they were old friends! Andy withdrew his hand sharply and glared at the witch doctor. He couldn't play along with this charade any longer.

Bob noticed Andy's reaction. He folded his arms and gave Andy an appraising look. "You don't understand the game, do you, son?"

"What game?" Andy demanded. He gestured around the temple ruins. "I don't understand any of this! All I know is that you shrank my grandfather's head and were working with his enemies. You obviously knew Professor Phink!"

Bob shook his head and chuckled, acting as if he were talking to a small child who couldn't understand a larger concept. "Andy—May I call you Andy?"

"No," said Andy.

Bungalow Bob moved closer and put an arm on Andy's shoulder. Andy stiffened and glared back at him. Bungalow Bob continued, saying, "Andy, your grandfather and I share a passion. We collect magical artifacts. And we collectors are known to go to extreme lengths to get what we want."

The witch doctor gestured to the temple. "This temple, for instance, was once inhabited by a very powerful cult. One that worshipped the Eternal Tree, the roots of which extend all the way here. It is a place of very powerful magic and one which suits my needs perfectly . . . for you see, I never intend to die. I am already over five hundred years old and still have much I wish to accomplish."

Andy gaped. "Wait, you know about the Eternal Tree?" he asked.

Bob looked at him with a quizzical expression. "Why, of course I do. Do you really suppose that I would choose a life underground in this crumbling ruin unless there were a good reason for it?" Understanding suddenly flashed on Bungalow Bob's craggy features, and he smiled. "Of course. You're looking for it, aren't you? And all this time I was drawing you to me, you had no idea that I had access to the tree. How ironic!" He chuckled.

"What do you mean, *drawing* us to you? We fell into this place by accident!" said Dotty.

Bob held up a long finger. "I don't believe in accidents, my dear." He snapped his fingers. A low growl emanated from somewhere in the ruins behind him. Then, to Andy and the others' surprise, two huge Bengal tigers with glowing red eyes appeared behind the witch doctor. Andy took an involuntary step backward. The beasts looked just as strange and ferocious as they had when he'd encountered one of them earlier.

But he was thrown off guard when Bob began scratching the closest one under the chin, just like an ordinary house cat.

"You might recognize my pets. I have several others, too, including a Dingonek."

Andy wasn't sure, but he thought he saw Rusty clench his one good hand into a tight fist at the mention of the name of the beast that had taken his other appendage.

"Wonderful creatures. Magically summoned, of course. I had them act like sheepdogs, herding you along in this direction until you fell right into my trap.

And how did I do it?" His teeth flashed in a triumphant grin. "With an ancient magical artifact, one that was believed lost, called the Beastcaller. I had to pay dearly to obtain it, but it is truly one of the gems of my collection. Which brings me back to my earlier mentioning of Professor Phink . . ."

Bungalow Bob paced in front of the group, growing animated. "The late professor offered me a certain artifact: a ring that could make the wearer turn into a fifty-foot-tall giant. A wonderful item! It was offered in exchange for reducing Ned Lostmore to his . . . er . . . current state."

"In other words, he paid you to shrink Grandfather's head," said Andy flatly.

"Precisely," said Bungalow Bob. "And I was supposed to be allowed to keep him in my collection! What an offer! You see, the magical properties of shrunken heads fuel my research. Their magic protects me from some of the dark curses associated with items that would normally carry with them too great a cost to use."

He spread his arms in a broad, all-encompassing gesture. "I am nothing more than a collector, a doctor, a man of science who gathers magical artifacts for his own personal research. So does your grandfather. I have my own reasons for gathering them, as does he. We have vastly different ideas about how to use these items, but bottom line, we're simply friendly competitors."

"I don't see anything friendly about shrinking someone's head," growled Rusty.

"Ah, well, that's just part of the game," said the witch doctor. "One which you'll soon be part of! Come, follow me. . . ."

Bungalow Bob wheeled around and walked inside the temple. Andy was amazed at how Bob acted like everything was simply a game of checkers! But Andy knew that his grandfather's life had been part of the stakes, and whatever his "game" was, it could be deadly.

However, seeing no other option at the moment, the group cautiously followed the doctor through a nearby doorway. Andy made sure his Zoomwriter was firmly in hand but tried not to grip it too tight as he trailed after the others down a narrow, twisting staircase.

They descended for several minutes, and the farther down they went, the darker and more oppressive the temple became. A flickering green light illuminated the slimy walls, and when they finally reached the bottom, Andy was surprised to see that the entire room was lit by torches that blazed with emerald fire.

The old man spread his arms wide and then brought his hands together with a resounding clap. The fire blazed even brighter, revealing walls filled with tiny alcoves . . . alcoves that each contained something horribly recognizable.

"Shrunken heads!" exclaimed Andy.

Bungalow Bob smiled. "Yes. My collection." He gestured proudly to the countless shelves. "Some were great, some were not. But all have a place of honor in my temple. In fact, there was only one that I ever *lost* . . . and it was one that I wanted far *more* than the others."

He grinned, baring rows of rather pointed teeth at

his wordplay. Andy grimaced. The very thought that this was the same sorcerer who had shrunk his grandfather's head was still staggering and almost too horrifying to believe.

It had always made Andy uncomfortable to think that such a bizarre ritual, which defied all science and reason, could have taken place. It had ruined Ned Lostmore's life in a way, but the ever resourceful and optimistic doctor had found a way to keep on living anyway.

"Well, if you're asking which one of us wants to go first to have our heads shrunk, I don't think you're going to get any volunteers," said Abigail. Her arms were crossed and she glared at him with a defiant expression.

Bungalow Bob sighed, looking disappointed. "Well, you do look like a sickly lot," he said, eyeing their black spots and gruesome pallor. "I would think it would feel much better to be shrunken and healthy than in your current state."

He moved closer. "And had one of you stepped forward, I could have rewarded you with special magical attributes. You could have served me in a position of great honor." He shrugged. "But now . . . well . . ."

And before anyone had time to react, the sorcerer picked up a small jungle totem from a nearby table. Then a bolt of mystical green fire spurted from the tiny statue, arcing toward Rusty Bucketts. The big pilot took the brunt of the magical blast directly in the face.

Then it happened. Andy watched in horror as Rusty's startled expression grew smaller as his entire head began to reduce in size . . . shrinking before their very eyes. A thick mist surrounded his legs and torso, and in moments they had completely vanished. In seconds, all that remained was a horribly small version of Rusty's head, lying on the floor. It was perfect in every detail, right down to the bushy red mustache.

Rusty's eyes were wide and more frightened than Andy had ever seen them. With a flick of his wrist, the witch doctor motioned to Rusty's tiny head and it rose magically from the floor and into the air, floated across the room, and landed neatly in an empty alcove.

"I'll get you for this!" Rusty shouted. His normally confident, booming voice sounded small and shaky, as if he'd swallowed a bunch of helium from a balloon.

Bungalow Bob turned to the others and shrugged. His smile reminded Andy of a little boy who had just been caught doing a bit of mischief. "Not to worry. His head will be put to great use. You see, shrunken heads with low intellect, like your friend's here, have a surprising amount of concentrated magical power. His is a wonderful addition to my collection. An interesting specimen."

"You have no right . . ." sputtered Andy. A wave of anger overtook him and he felt like he would do anything to stop the sorcerer. On impulse, he raised his Zoomwriter and aimed—

But Bungalow Bob had only to flick the tip of his finger in Andy's general direction, and the normally thunderous blast from the Zoomwriter's atomic pulse emitter never happened. The pen just gave off a small, light hiss that died quickly. Andy stared down at it with a panicked expression.

The old witch doctor tut-tutted and slowly shook his head. "You really mustn't try to fight me. There is nothing you possess that could have the slightest effect." Then, with another quick flick of his wrist, Betty and Dotty's favorite weapons were removed from the pouches at their belts. The sisters watched helplessly as a constellation of their razor-sharp throwing stars floated into the air and stacked neatly on a very high shelf.

The twins' expressions went from surprised to furious. But, like Andy, they could do nothing. It seemed to all of them that the inevitable was about to happen whether they wanted it to or not. They were all going to end up as batteries to fuel this sorcerer's power, and there was nothing they could do about it. Soon, Andy would be like his grandfather in more than just character.

Soon, he would need a cabinet of his own.

Flash! A second burst of green fire flew from the sorcerer's totem and Betty and Dotty were subjected to the same reduction that Rusty had recently undergone, separated from their joined body for the first time in their lives. It all happened so fast that Andy could hardly believe it when he saw the sisters' heads in alcoves positioned right next to Rusty's. They were screaming bloody murder, which only added to the horror of the situation.

Andy knew if he didn't think of something fast, he would be right there with them. He glanced around the room, desperately seeking some way out of their predicament.

Suddenly, a chime sounded. Andy clenched his fists, preparing for whatever pain was about to come next. But his eyes widened when, after a long moment, nothing happened.

His gaze settled on a gigantic hourglass with hour markings etched on its surface. The Doomsday Device had struck. Why hadn't it affected them?

Bungalow Bob grinned, knowing Andy's thoughts. "The Doomsday Device has no effect on me, or you, while you are in my temple. The magic I possess is greater than that any artifact could generate."

He twiddled his fingers. Andy and the others felt

a light breeze wash over them. When Andy glanced down, he noticed that all the marks of the plague were gone from his arms.

Bungalow Bob chuckled when he saw their stunned expressions. "I hate imperfect specimens."

The witch doctor had raised the jungle totem again and was pointing his bony fingers in Abigail's direction, about to shrink her head, when on a sudden impulse Andy shouted, "Stop!"

The old sorcerer started. "And why should I?" he asked after a pause.

"Because . . ." Andy paused, his mind racing furiously. "I have a deal to make with you."

The witch doctor smiled in amusement. "And just what could you offer me besides your head?"

"My . . . head . . . is exactly what I'm talking about," Andy said, thinking fast. Then he straightened, looking Bungalow Bob directly in the eye. "I challenge you to a battle of wits. If I win, we get to go free, and if you win, you get our heads."

Bungalow Bob laughed. "I could just take them anyway. You do realize that, don't you?"

Andy said nothing but continued to stare defiantly at the old man. Finally, Bungalow Bob shrugged and grinned.

"Why not? I haven't had any amusement in a long time," said Bob. "But you might regret it. I hold degrees from all the major universities, both in medicine and the paranormal sciences."

Andy didn't flinch. He knew it was a desperate play and had doubted it would work. But thankfully, the old man seemed amenable to the idea. Bob motioned for Andy to follow him, and as Andy did, he noticed that they were heading deeper into the temple toward a large stone door. When they drew close, Andy noticed that it was covered with tangled vines and ancient carvings. Bungalow Bob stopped and stroked the door affectionately. Then, turning to Andy, he said, "Behind this door lies a challenging maze unlike any you've ever faced. In years past, I would test my potential protégés with its mental challenges to see who might be worthy to stand at my side."

He gestured broadly. "And as you can see, I have no protégés. Unfortunately, they all failed my test. If you succeed, and I hope you will, you might join me! I could really use an assistant. Imagine the possibilities!"

Andy gritted his teeth. *I'd rather die*, he thought.

Bungalow Bob grinned at what he apparently mistook for a determined expression on Andy's face. "I can see you're eager to get started. Good! Well, know this . . . no matter how my little test turns out, it won't be a total waste. The heads of all the others who tried and failed made valuable additions to my collection." His blue eyes narrowed, flashing dangerously. "And if you fail, yours will, too."

Andy gulped as the heavy door swung inward and he saw the darkness that lay beyond it. A dank smell wafted out from the hidden recess, and he had the eerie feeling he used to get as a small boy when he'd been about to enter the haunted house at a carnival.

He remembered just how much he hated haunted houses.

Then, steeling himself, he stepped forward. And as he moved past Bungalow Bob, the old witch doctor said, "Oh, I forgot to mention—there are terrible monsters in that maze that haven't been fed in weeks. Also, there are weapons scattered about, but you can only earn them by solving my puzzles. There, you've been given a clue. I'm not so unreasonable, am I?"

Andy didn't even glance up as he walked through the door. In his opinion, Bungalow Bob was absolutely anything but reasonable. But instead of saying so, he simply mumbled, "Thanks for the tip," and walked inside.

The next thing he knew, his world was plunged into total darkness as the heavy door swung shut behind him.

Chapter Sixteen
The Maze

Andy felt forward in the darkness, hoping to find something solid. Taking a few hesitant steps forward, he felt his fingers brush against a wall.

At least it's not slimy, Andy thought. He had no idea what was waiting for him in the maze, but somehow it would have been worse if the wall had been covered with some kind of wet or sticky substance that he couldn't see.

And please don't let there be any mummies. Please, please, please...

Even though he was far from Egypt and the pyramids, there was a chance Bungalow Bob had an artifact that could summon one—and Andy certainly didn't want to go through that horrifying experience again!

Andy moved his feet close to the base of the wall, thinking that if there were any pits or traps in front of him, he had a better chance of avoiding them if he stayed close to it. He walked with one foot placed directly in front of the other, creeping slowly and testing with his toe at each step.

It might take me a while, but he didn't say anything about a time limit. Better safe than sorry.

Test. Step. Test. Step.

He proceeded this way for several minutes. Even though his eyes had had time to adjust to the darkness, he still wasn't able to see a thing.

Perhaps it's magic, Andy thought. But that thought made him feel even more worried about the "monsters"

Bungalow Bob had mentioned. If they were magical creatures, what kind of weapons would be needed to kill them?

He decided that it was best to try to just take on each challenge as it presented itself and forced himself to stay focused.

After a few more minutes of walking, he came to his first turn. He felt the corners of the stone wall with his fingers, probing as he went along. While he was feeling his way, his hand brushed against something sticking out of the stones. Andy carefully felt along its surface.

"It's a switch," he said aloud, startled by the discovery. It reminded him of the one he'd found back at the pyramid, but it was a bit different in size and structure. He realized with a start that it felt just like a light switch! He was about to push on it when he paused.

His first thought had been that the switch would turn on the lights. *But what if it's only made to make a person think that? People don't like to be in the dark. What could be a more welcome discovery than a light switch?*

Andy lowered his hand. As much as he wanted to flick the switch, some instinct told him that it was far too convenient and obvious.

"I'll bet it isn't a light switch at all. In fact, I bet it would set off some kind of a trap. Not going to do that," he whispered. "Got to stay sharp!"

And with mixed feelings he moved onward, fearing the dark but feeling some kind of inward certainty that he'd successfully passed the first test.

He followed the corridor as it wound around to the right. Whenever he was presented with the option of turning left, he reasoned that it would be better to stick to the right in hopes that it would eventually lead him out of the maze. He'd read somewhere that if one followed this rule from the entry point of a maze, the probability of finding one's way out increased substantially.

He'd been proceeding this way cautiously for some time when his toe bumped something hard on the floor in front of him. Reaching down very carefully, he tentatively touched the object.

I wonder what that is, Andy thought. For a minute he considered what to do. It might, of course, be a trap. But since the witch doctor had mentioned that there were also things placed in the maze to help him, he felt that he had no choice but to investigate it.

Andy picked it up. The object felt cool and smooth, like a flat piece of metal that was about six inches square. It also had irregular blocks cut out of its surface. Although he couldn't for the life of him figure out what it was for, he couldn't help feeling he'd found something worth keeping. Since it was too big to pocket, he slipped it underneath his shirt and continued forward.

He hadn't gone more than ten steps when a flicker of light down a passageway on his right caught his attention. After he'd spent so much time in the dark, it flared with an incandescent brightness that seemed much more powerful than it really was.

A candle!

Relief washed over him. He felt like primitive man as he gazed at the small light, glad that it could chase away the dangerous shadows and unknown dangers that lurked in the darkness.

He wanted to run toward it. But once again, he fought his impulse and kept his head. He stared at the light and waited to see if there was any movement within the area of its glow.

And he was glad he did.

After about five minutes of waiting, a shadow flicked past the wall. Andy couldn't tell exactly what made it, but it looked like some kind of large claw or mandible.

There's something waiting near that candle.

He shuddered. Andy knew that whatever it was, it was certainly going to be dangerous. He wondered what the "monsters" Bungalow Bob had mentioned would look like.

He said there would be weapons, too, Andy thought. *I wonder where they are.*

He gazed around, looking to see if he could find any clues. For some time he didn't notice anything unusual. The feeble light didn't do much to illuminate the wall in his immediate vicinity. But after a few more minutes of searching, he spotted something at the bottom of the wall across from where he was crouching.

It appeared to be a small tube or cylinder, just visible where the shadows of the wall met the first bit of light thrown by the candle.

Stepping carefully and quietly, he crept across to the other side, hoping all the while that he wouldn't alert whatever monster hid near the candle to his presence.

He reached the small cylinder without incident and, after picking it up, found that the cap on its end could open. He reached inside and withdrew its contents.

A scroll?

Andy tilted the paper in the direction of the candle flame and could just barely make out the writing upon it.

> *Three kittens without mittens went up the hill,*
> *and placed three stones into a well.*
> *Up goes Jack and down falls Jill,*
> *Two kittens come tumbling after.*

Humpty fell from the edge
onto the stones below.
But all turned right on the fateful night,
As all children surely know.

"Complete nonsense!" Andy whispered quietly. But he recognized some of the references in the poem as Mother Goose rhymes, so at least that was something.

There's something here . . . but what is it?

He reread the lines of the poem. But as he tried to make sense of the writing, he just ended up confusing himself more. What in the world could kittens, Jack and Jill, and Humpty Dumpty have to do with the situation he was in? He tried rearranging the words, hoping they might be a code of some kind.

They weren't.

He reversed the letters, hoping they might spell something backward.

Nothing.

After several minutes of this, he was suddenly

startled by the gong of the Potentate's Doomsday Device. He flinched automatically, but was relieved to find that Bungalow Bob's magic still kept him from feeling any effects.

But the chime did do something. Perhaps it was because it distracted him from his train of thought, but suddenly a new idea occurred to him. He looked down at the paper, measuring its size with his eyes.

Then he withdrew the metal plate he'd found from beneath his shirt and laid it directly on top of the page.

It fit perfectly.

And better still, Andy suddenly knew the reason for the carved holes in the plate. When laid directly on the sheet, the plate covered certain words and revealed others, sending him a clear message:

> **Three** kittens without mittens went up the hill,
> and placed three **stones** into a well.
> **Up** goes Jack and down falls Jill,
> **Two** kittens come tumbling after.

*Humpty fell **from the edge***
onto the stones below.
*But all **turned right** on the fateful night,*
As all children surely know.

Andy glanced at the place at the bottom of the wall where he'd found the scroll. *Three stones up, two from the edge. Turn right.* Feeling excited, he counted three stones up and then counted in two more from the edge of the wall.

"Turn right," he whispered.

And reaching out to the stone that he'd located, he placed his palm against it and turned his hand clockwise.

There was a small pop, and the stone fell out of the wall into Andy's hand. Looking inside the spot where it had been, Andy was immensely relieved to see the hilt of a small dagger waiting inside.

He removed it and examined it in the dim light. It was beautifully made, and its edges gleamed.

Andy glanced back at the candle. Whatever was waiting there for him was going to get a surprise.

He rose from his crouched position and, clenching the dagger tightly in his hand, moved slowly forward on the balls of his feet.

Come and get it.

Chapter Seventeen
The Scorpupine

The candle was standing on a large, somewhat rickety table that blocked any further progress down the right side of the maze. And as Andy drew closer, little by little he was able to make out more of the shadowy something that he'd seen earlier. The monster was hiding underneath the table, crouching there and waiting for its victim. He couldn't quite tell its shape, but Andy noticed a pair of dark eyes glittering in the shadows and a strange insect-like clicking sound.

Andy shuddered and tried not to think of all the creepy-crawly things he hated. He raised his knife, displaying it where the eyes beneath the table could see it, and said in as brave a voice as he could muster, "Let me pass!"

The strange clicking grew agitated. And then the thing began to move, scuttling slowly into the candlelight and revealing its hideous form for the first time.

Andy involuntarily drew back a step. His face grew slack with horror and his eyes were wide. He'd never seen such a thing!

Its body was covered with sharp spikes and its muzzle was vaguely mammalian. The eyes were dark and intelligent. But the monster also possessed a wicked-looking ebony tail that curved over its back like a scorpion's and had matching, huge razor-sharp claws. These latter appendages were responsible for the clicking noises that Andy had heard earlier, and they snapped like pliers as the creature advanced.

"Stay back!" Andy cried.

The monster stopped and gazed at Andy for a long moment. Then, to his surprise, it spoke in a high, raspy voice.

"I am the Scorpupine. Will you hear what I have to say?"

Andy was taken aback. He hadn't expected to be questioned by the creature. Once again, his instinct was to protect himself, to attack the horrible thing or run away. But like before, Andy felt that by operating with logic rather than feeling, he might have a chance to beat the maze.

"All right," Andy said in a slightly quavery voice. "Tell me."

The terrifying creature drew a breath and then began to recite,

"Threaten me at your peril,
My sting it never fails,
My claws are iron vises,
And dead men tell no tales.

"If you would win and save your life,
Your blade will not suffice,
For my armor never will be cut
No matter how sharp the knife.

"Quickly you must find a way,
Or prepare to meet your grave,
But cross the line and take a fall,
And only then will you be saved."

Andy stared, trying to think about what he'd just heard. Although he'd been listening intently, he needed to hear it again to try to sort it out.

It's another riddle, he surmised.

Gathering his courage, he asked, "Could you please repeat that?"

The Scorpupine did. But Andy noticed that while doing so it inched closer toward a clearly indicated demarcation line on the maze floor, one that was closer to where Andy was standing. It was a circle of stones that had been embedded around the circumference of the table, about three or four feet from the table's edges.

Andy tried not to panic. Seeing the creature come closer was terrifying. But he forced himself instead to repeat the rhyme in his head and work on sorting out what it meant.

Threaten me at your peril,
My sting it never fails,
My claws are iron vises,
And dead men tell no tales.

That part seemed fairly simple. But there was one line that stood out in Andy's mind: *Dead men tell no tales.*

Sounds like something a pirate would say, Andy thought. He, of course, had read *Treasure Island* several times and knew most of the book by heart. He thought about the second verse.

If you would win and save your life
Your blade will not suffice,
For my armor never will be cut
No matter how sharp the knife.

Well, that seems self-explanatory, too, Andy thought. *Of course, it could be lying to get me to let my guard down.* He glanced at the glittering knife he'd found. If it wasn't for fighting the monster, then what was it for? It was just too convenient that the monster would mention a blade in the rhyme if it didn't have significance. It had to mean something more than stating the obvious.

Andy blew out a breath and, after running a hand through his sandy hair, considered the third verse.

Quickly you must find a way,
Or prepare to meet your grave,
But cross the line and take a fall,
And only then will you be saved.

Out of all the verses, this one seemed the most cryptic and the most important. He didn't like the *Quickly you must find a way / Or prepare to meet your grave* part, because that put the pressure on. How long did he actually have to solve the puzzle?

He glanced at the beast and noticed that while he'd been thinking, it had pressed even closer and was now perched right at the edge of the line. It was only a couple of feet from where he stood. Andy didn't know whether or not the stones that separated him from the monster would keep it at bay, but he also didn't want to wait too long to find out.

But cross the line and take a fall,
And only then will you be saved.

Andy glanced at the line that separated them. He didn't like the sound of what that phrase implicated. Could it really be suggesting that he step over the line and fall down in front of the Scorpupine, giving up like a dog that had been beaten by a bigger one?

It certainly seems that way, Andy thought grimly. The creature's eyes bored into Andy's own as if it were trying to read what he was thinking. The large pincers snapped. Instinctively, Andy knew that he didn't have much time left.

He had just resolved to take a step closer to the monster when he suddenly remembered something.

Dead men tell no tales. . . . Cross the line.

There was a connection there. In nautical terms, a "line" was a rope on a ship. Could "crossing the line" mean something else?

He glanced around the walls and noticed something that he hadn't before. Because of the candle on the table and the monster beneath it, his eyes had been automatically drawn downward. But just above him, tied around a hook, was a rope. It disappeared into a hole in the wall.

The monster clicked its claws with agitation. The stinger on its tail rose into the air. Andy glanced down at his knife and suddenly realized that "crossing the line" with the blade could mean cutting the rope.

The monster seemed to guess what Andy was thinking and charged forward, its deadly claws raised and its stinger poised to strike! Andy quickly swiped at the rope, severing it in two.

With a sharp click, a hidden trapdoor opened beneath his feet and he was suddenly tumbling down into the darkness. The stinger of the Scorpupine thudded into the lid of the trapdoor, missing Andy by an inch.

When he hit the bottom, it was with some relief that he found there was a straw mattress placed there to cushion his landing. But his relief was short-lived when he looked around the dimly lit dungeon into which he'd fallen and saw what was scattered around him.

Skeletons!

He gazed at the piles of red skulls with revulsion.

Were they covered in blood? Then he noticed that on the other side of the room was a pile of blackened skulls, looking to Andy as if they'd been burned in a fire. He tried not to retch.

Then, with sudden clarity, he realized the import of his situation.

All these people must have failed Bungalow Bob's maze and never gotten out. Could it be that these were the other candidates for apprenticeship?

With dawning horror, Andy took in his surroundings. The trapdoor above him had closed again, and at first glance, it seemed as if there were no other way out.

The room, which was only about twelve feet wide by twelve feet across, was lit by a dim phosphorescent glow. The floor was the most unusual part of the cell. It was divided into a grid pattern of dark and pale tiles and looked very dirty and unkempt.

Please, let there be a clue or something! he thought desperately. The whole thing didn't make sense! He knew that he'd been clever in figuring out the monster's riddle. Why, then, had he ended up here, at an apparent dead end?

After searching the entire cell for a way out, he came to a grim conclusion. "This is it," he said softly. "I'm going to be down here forever, trapped like those guys." He glanced over at the skulls.

He sat down and thought about Bungalow Bob and his strange obsession. How could anyone treat people's lives with such a cavalier attitude? It seemed like everything was some kind of sick game to the old witch doctor.

And then, with sudden clarity, a light popped on in Andy's head. He chuckled quietly to himself. Of course. The answer was so simple it was almost childish.

Feeling certain that he'd figured it out, Andy moved over to the two piles of skulls. Looking at each one closely, he was relieved to see that the red ones weren't covered with blood, and the black ones weren't burned.

It was paint.

Andy gathered the red skulls and arranged them

in two neat rows, placing one skull on each of the alternating-color tiles at the back of one side of the room. Then he did the same with the black skulls on the opposite side.

When the rows were complete, he stared down at the giant-size checkerboard he'd created. He didn't have to wait long after that for something to happen. Slowly, almost majestically, a red skull from the first row rose into the air and moved a single square toward the black side.

The game had begun.

Andy liked checkers. But he soon found that this game was like none other—for, if Andy was jumped by his invisible opponent, the entire tile disappeared along with the skull resting on it, opening a gap in the floor that went down, down, down into nothingness.

Andy didn't want to know what would happen if he made too many mistakes. The thought that the floor he stood upon could disappear made his knees weak. When he went to advance one of his skulls, he tiptoed across the board, fearing that at any time one of the squares might open beneath him and he would find himself falling into an endless pit!

During the tense game, Andy found that he made very few mistakes after his first one. He only missed one other opportunity—a move that crowned his opponent, who had moved into his back row. When it happened, Andy was standing directly next to the tile that disappeared and watched, horrified, as the white square tumbled down into the infinite blackness.

He shuddered and continued the game. Fortunately, he had no further incidents. Finally, at the end of the game, Andy executed a magnificent triple jump on his invisible opponent and couldn't help shouting "Yes!" when he saw both piles of skulls reappear where they had been when he'd first discovered them.

Then, like a fog disappearing before a blazing sun, the walls around him evaporated into thin air and he found himself standing back in the temple in front of Bungalow Bob. The witch doctor's face showed astonishment. But then, to Andy's surprise, his face crinkled into an amused smile.

"You've beaten me, Andy Stanley," he said. "Which only shows that both you and your grandfather have exceeded my expectations."

Chapter Eighteen
Ned's Reason

With a simple flick of his wrist, Bungalow Bob restored Rusty, Betty, and Dotty back to their previous forms, much to their collective relief.

"Blast and burn that witch doctor," cursed Rusty. "I've never felt so small-minded."

Andy chuckled. "You sound like Grandfather," he said.

Rusty, as always, was the last to see the humor. He just stared at Andy, confused, as if he didn't know he'd said anything remotely funny. Andy grinned and shook his head. Some things never changed.

Turning to Bungalow Bob, Andy asked, "Why was my grandfather here, anyway?"

The witch doctor's expression turned sour. "It wasn't to consult with me about magical cures, I'll tell you that much." He leveled his gaze at Andy. "He was searching for magical artifacts. He was using an interesting pair of boots at the time, ones that always led the wearer toward sources of magic. Those boots led him here, and now they are in my collection. He lost them fair and square. . . ."

Without saying more, Bob motioned for them to follow. Andy walked next to the witch doctor as he led the group from the room filled with shrunken heads down a twisting stone hallway that led inside the darkest recesses of the crumbling temple. As they descended several sloping hallways, the air around them seemed to get thicker and more humid. And when they finally reached the end of the hall, Andy saw the reason why.

An underground river was lapping at the stone banks. And beside the banks was anchored an unusual boat. It had obviously been designed by sorcery, because it glowed with its own mystical light.

"All aboard," Bungalow Bob said and motioned for them to step inside the boat. Andy noticed that the small boat's seats were positioned so that the passengers in front and back both faced forward. There was no motor or way of steering it that he could see.

"I would suggest that you keep your hands and arms inside the boat at all times. The water that this boat floats upon is filled with a particularly deadly species of piranha."

And then, with a flick of Bob's hand, the boat immediately began to move downriver.

The water was so dark it almost looked black. Soon, the stone dock gave way to earthen banks upon which strange dark trees grew upside down. Andy took note of the unusual plants with their trunks that stretched upward to the high dirt ceiling, their roots presumably emerging somewhere aboveground. Big juicy oranges grew on their underground branches, and Andy couldn't help remembering the similar tree he'd seen when he and Abigail had found each other in the jungle.

At that time, he'd seen nothing but the tree's roots. But seeing the full treetops flourishing underground filled him with curiosity. How it was possible that an orange tree could grow and bear fruit in a place like this, a damp tunnel of earth and stone with no sun?

"Those aren't actually oranges," Bungalow Bob said, noticing where Andy was looking. "It is a very unusual type of fruit known to the learned as the Citrus Star. It has mild magical properties, such as granting the taster purple skin and golden eyes. It has also been known to cure the common cold."

Andy nodded in reply. He'd forgotten that magic could take the place of reason when something could not be explained any other way.

As they floated farther downriver, he noticed a

beautiful brick terrace that was positioned on a nearby bank. Tables and chairs were gathered around a large platform, and the walls were covered with ornately painted masks and artwork. It looked like a rather nice place to entertain company . . . something friendly and definitely out of place when Andy considered the grim temple.

"What's that place?" asked Abigail.

"Ah, *that*, ladies and gentlemen, is my Tahitian Terrace. I used to entertain kings, queens, the highest-ranking magicians, sorceresses, magi, and alchemists there. They came seeking my knowledge and protection. I knew them all. Yen Sid, Merlin . . . they all were here at one point or another."

The old man's gaze grew distant at the memory. Andy noticed that the terrace was very clean and that there was a simple broom sweeping lazily at some dust, seemingly of its own magical accord.

Fireflies danced around the bank of the river as the cavern in which they traveled narrowed down to a stone tunnel and soon grew so dark that Andy couldn't see his hand in front of his face.

Whoosh! A gust of air hit Andy as the boat suddenly plunged down a small but steep waterfall. It caught Andy and the others off guard, and even Abigail let out a little squeal (which, in Andy's opinion, was rather unusual for her).

When the boat leveled out, they all found themselves in an illuminated cavern. Colored lights from an unknown source flickered on the walls, producing a beautiful but eerie effect.

Bungalow Bob directed the boat to stop at a small dock. Andy and the group stepped out of the boat and followed him to a small door so carefully crafted that it seemed to blend directly into the cavern wall itself.

"Clever," said Betty.

"Impressive," added Dotty.

Both of the assassins obviously appreciated secretive hiding places from which a person could attack without being observed.

Bungalow Bob didn't seem to notice. His face was fixed with an expression of fierce pride, but Andy wondered if there was a little bit of concern there as well. It seemed pretty evident that the witch doctor seldom had company in recent years and that showing guests around was something of a novelty. Andy wondered if he'd grown so used to his lonely existence that it felt like a bit of an intrusion to share his inner sanctum with strangers.

"Now, this is something that not many people have ever seen," said Bungalow Bob. "As you've witnessed, I enjoy collecting things."

"We noticed," said Rusty Bucketts, massaging his neck.

"Andy Stanley, the objects behind this door were of particular interest to your grandfather," said Bungalow Bob. "It is the reason he sought me out, and also the reason the Collective wanted me to trap him here. I don't usually allow guests to see this area of my temple, but these are extenuating circumstances."

Bungalow Bob clapped his hands together and the door swung open. Andy felt a surge of curiosity and anticipation as they walked inside. As they passed the doorframe, the darkened room was suddenly illuminated by a bright green glow. Andy gazed around at what he saw in complete awe. Situated on every available table, bench, shelf, and chair were artifacts the like of which Andy and the others had never seen before.

"Wow," said Abigail quietly.

Bungalow Bob beamed with pride and motioned for them to follow him to a nearby table where an object that looked like a small coffin was positioned.

"Let's start with this one. This is my Sar-*cough*-agus. I found this rare item in a Phoenician tomb. Upon opening that lid"—he indicated the lid of the coffin—"I can effectively wipe out almost a third of the jungle population with a terrible consumptive sickness. Out with the old, in with the new!" he quipped.

Andy leaned close to Abigail and whispered, "Definitely a psychopath."

She nodded grimly. "We need to be careful," she mouthed back.

"And over here is my hurricane creator."

The others oohed and aahed as the sorcerer led them through the rest of the room. Abigail suddenly noticed something perched on a nearby pedestal and ran over to it with an excited expression. She pointed at the object and said, "Andy, look! That's the Hand of the Kraken! Everyone in the J.E.S. told me it had been lost at sea!"

Bungalow Bob hardly had time to comment before Abigail had dashed to a second pillar, this one with a small carved kangaroo placed upon it. To Andy, it almost looked like a child's toy.

"The Jarjum. It will age a person thirty years at a single touch!" Abigail looked so excited that she seemed about to touch it herself. The others were all feeling as astounded as she was.

"Besides the J.E.S. headquarters, I have to say that there are more powerful artifacts here than I've ever seen in one place!" exclaimed Rusty. "No wonder Ned came looking for them."

"Precisely," said Bungalow Bob. "And once I found that he was considering taking them from me, I decided to shrink his head."

"I'm sure he wasn't going to steal them," Andy began, sticking up for his grandfather. "Once he found that you had them in your collection, he would have offered you a trade or something."

Bungalow Bob gave him a suspicious look. "So you say," the witch doctor said, "but I'm not one to take any chances."

"Neither is he," agreed Andy. "Do you know anything about the J.E.S. and what we stand for?"

"I know that you have a, shall we say, fondness for rare artifacts of power," said Bob.

"There's more to it than that," Abigail chimed in. "Our whole purpose is to keep them safe from the Potentate and her Collective. If they ever found what you have here"—she motioned to the room filled with antiquities—"they'd attack. There would be so many of those cutthroats at your door, you couldn't shrink all their heads at once."

Bungalow Bob straightened and, after folding his arms, glared down at Abigail. "The entire reason that they don't 'attack,' as you say, is because between my proximity to the Eternal Tree, my shrunken heads, and my artifact collection, I could repel any attempt with more magic than the Potentate could possibly imagine!"

"But that's the whole point to the Potentate having the Doomsday Device," explained Andy. "She's trying to eliminate the Jungle Explorers' Society so that she can steal all our artifacts. She wants to take over the world! If she gets the J.E.S. artifacts, she'll have enough power to confront even the likes of you."

Bungalow Bob looked thoughtful. After a moment, he spoke. "I knew that she had the Doomsday Device. Hmm. So that's her plan, eh? Well, I'm unwilling to allow that."

Rusty turned from the table where he was inspecting

a strange artifact on a chain that looked like a mummified lizard's head. "What are you saying? Whose side are you on?"

"Nobody's *side*," the witch doctor grunted. "But I can't allow one person to keep me from locating more items for my collection. If she were in control, then I would have my work cut out for me. She wouldn't have anyone standing between her and whatever artifacts remained for the finding."

The witch doctor seemed to have come to a decision. Turning to Andy, he asked, "Before you stumbled upon my temple, where were you trying to go?"

"We were looking for a leprechaun named Patrick Begorra. He supposedly resides in the oldest tree on Earth, one that is almost impossible to find. My grandfather said that he possesses knowledge that will help us stop the Doomsday Device."

"Well, I've never heard of such a person myself," Bungalow Bob confessed. "However, if he resides in the Eternal Tree, I believe I can help you locate him." The old man walked over to a large armoire that was carved with figures of flying snails. He opened the doors and took a folded piece of parchment from a drawer inside.

"This artifact is called the Finders' Map. It can locate anything the searcher is looking for if asked. Locating the leprechaun would be impossible for most magicians and extremely taxing for even one such as I. But with this artifact, even the impossible is possible."

The witch doctor waved his hand over the parchment and murmured a magic word. Suddenly, lines appeared all over the parchment where there had been none before.

Andy and Abigail stared down at it. For the life of him, Andy couldn't make heads or tails of the scribbles upon it.

"They're roots!" Abigail suddenly said. "That's not a linear map. Those are tree roots!"

"Brava," said the sorcerer. "These are the roots of the Eternal Tree. They stretch deep underground and cover nearly the entire planet. Such a map would be of priceless value if it were discovered by the right person."

"But how does it help us?" asked Andy. "With so many roots, how could we ever know how to follow the one closest to us to the tree itself?"

Bungalow Bob smiled. "That's where your jujus come in handy." He pointed at the jujus hanging around Betty's and Dotty's necks, one shaped like a tree and the other shaped like an eye. "Used together, the juju of discovery should show the pathway, and the juju of knowledge should show the precise location of what you seek."

He spread his arms wide. "When you use them in conjunction with the map, even the leprechaun cannot keep himself hidden."

Andy and Abigail exchanged glances. Then Abigail took the two jujus from Betty and Dotty, who turned them over willingly. Holding them in her hands, she marched back over to the map.

"Take us to what we seek," she said.

And the lines on the map that led to the Eternal Tree suddenly began to glow.

Chapter Nineteen
The Plan

"We're in for it now," Rusty grumbled.

Andy had to agree. The plan they'd come up with was going to stretch them all to their limits. He only hoped they would survive.

While Andy and Abigail sought Patrick Begorra and hoped to obtain knowledge that would destroy the Doomsday Device, Rusty, Betty, and Dotty would join Bungalow Bob in battling the Potentate. If they could use Bob's magic artifacts, they might be able to surprise the Potentate and clear the way for Andy and Abigail to get to the Doomsday Device and destroy it.

"Now, just to be clear, I don't want to risk losing any of my artifacts to my enemies, is that understood?" Bob said sternly. "Those working with me must use them under my direct supervision."

Everyone nodded in solemn agreement. Andy knew that Bob wasn't helping them out of the goodness of his heart. Protecting his artifact collection was obviously the only thing that mattered.

They stood at the edge of the docks from where they had journeyed to the sorcerer's secret rooms. This time, instead of ushering them onto a boat, Bungalow Bob had taken five Persian rugs from his collection and laid them next to each other. Each was about the size of a doormat, but far more elegant. They were beautifully stitched with woven patterns of red, gold, and blue.

"These artifacts are magic carpets from Ali Baba's Cave of Wonders," Bungalow Bob said. "They've appeared in all kinds of stories, so don't be too disappointed when you try the real thing. They're not as maneuverable as a modern airplane and tend to act up quite a bit in air turbulence."

Rusty raised up his hand in a placating gesture. "Don't tell me about turbulence, old man," he said. "I've been a bush pilot all my life."

Instead of being offended, Bungalow Bob looked mildly amused. "Well, watch your stabilizers and hang on tight. By leaning left or right, you control the pitch and yaw . . . but I shouldn't have to tell an expert like yourself."

"Of course not," huffed Rusty, who still hadn't completely forgiven the sorcerer for shrinking his head.

"Oh, and I almost forgot," Bungalow Bob said as he reached into his pocket. He pulled out two rings and offered one each to Andy and Abigail.

"Because the others will be in my proximity, they won't be affected by the Doomsday Device. However, with the help of these rings, the same should apply to you. Each gemstone is an artifact of protection. Wonderful little treasures. They should provide you with the protection you need . . . at least temporarily," he added. "And, of course, I'll be wanting them back when you're done with them."

"Of course," replied Andy automatically.

Andy and Abigail both thanked him as they slipped the ornate rings onto their fingers.

"Now then, Mr. Bucketts, if you will please activate your juju's tracking," said the sorcerer.

Rusty removed the charm from around his neck but stared at it with a blank expression. He appeared unsure of how to activate it.

"Here, you big lug, let us have that," said Betty and Dotty in unison. After taking it, Dotty held it and instructed the juju in a commanding voice to find the Doomsday Device.

The elephant juju glowed in response. Then, to everyone's astonishment, a faint golden beam of light emerged from it, shining in a straight line to the south.

Rusty's face lit up with determination. "What are we waiting for?"

He leapt aboard one of the small carpets. Upon contact, the rug shot up into the air, following after the beam as a howling Rusty hung on for dear life.

"I guess that means we'd better all get going," said Andy.

Bungalow Bob nodded. "And may good luck find us all."

Chapter Twenty
Roots

When Andy and Abigail took to the air on the magic carpets, it felt to Andy like he was riding the most terrifying roller coaster he'd ever been on. In spite of Bungalow Bob's light instruction on how to control it, the carpet seemed to truly have a mind of its own.

Thankfully, simply hanging on and not falling off was enough to get them to the destination they'd asked it to find. And after nearly an hour of flying in deep tunnels under the earth, Andy was relieved to arrive at the most massive root structure he'd ever seen.

"Would you look at that?" Andy said, awestruck, as he shakily disembarked from his flying rug.

Abigail looked as if she'd fared much better than Andy, and she stepped off her carpet as nimbly as if she'd been flying them all her life. Growing up at sea with a boat captain for a father certainly had its advantages when it came to having good balance.

"It's unbelievable!" she said, impressed. Then she added, "Look!"

Andy saw where she was pointing. At the base of the root, which Andy guessed had to be at least twenty feet tall and thirty feet wide, was an opening. Moving closer, they saw that it had been carved into the root itself by some kind of tool. An elegant Celtic knot was carved above the doorway, an Irish decoration in an uncanny location.

"Must be the place," said Andy.

"Yeah," said Abigail. "Should we go inside?"

"Kungaloosh!" said Andy. Then he added, "After you . . ."

Abigail grinned and shot through the opening. Andy followed and, once inside, saw that the root itself was hollow. Small tendrils beneath their feet gave them something to grip as they climbed upward, and the two began to half walk, half climb inside the root, both of them hoping that the tree above wasn't too far away.

Walking inside a hollow root was a strange and rather creepy experience. The soft illumination inside the tunnel made Andy feel ill at ease and more than a little claustrophobic.

Abigail consulted the map. "I think we're supposed to go this way," she said, heading off to a gently twisting tunnel to the left.

No sooner had they taken a step in that direction than a bloodcurdling shriek ripped through the air. It made all the hair on Andy's arms and neck stand up.

"Maybe not," he said weakly.

Abigail looked as shaken by the sound as Andy was.

It wasn't the chime of the Doomsday Device, but it was nearly as bone jarring.

Abigail consulted the map a second time, then shook her head and said quietly, "I'm afraid so."

Andy reached into his pocket and removed his Zoomwriter. Taking a deep breath, he said, "Okay, well, it sounds to me like Patrick Begorra doesn't like visitors. We'll have to show him we mean business."

After about twenty feet, the root tunnel opened up into a huge cavern. The walls were made of the same material, but it was as if it had been magically stretched and pulled into a chamber so immense that it reminded Andy of a castle. Twisted tendrils grew up from the floor and down from the ceiling, resembling grasping claws. But worst of all, at the very end of the dark chamber was a ghostly horse and carriage.

"What's that?" breathed Abigail.

"No idea," said Andy. "But it doesn't look good."

The six horses that pulled the carriage had glowing red eyes. They pawed and stamped the ground, looking tortured and uncomfortable. Andy watched as the doors to the carriage slowly swung open and three terrible-looking figures emerged.

The first was man-shaped, tall, thin, and wearing a top hat and frock coat, but where his face should have been was only a formless gray mist.

The second figure was small and shriveled, a misshapen thing that snorted as it waddled from the carriage. To Andy it looked like some kind of crumpled ape. But the third one really made him cringe. It was nearly transparent, a dim reflection of a once-living woman wearing a white wedding dress. Her silver hair tumbled over her shoulders and eyes, and no sooner had Andy looked in her direction than she let out a second horrible, gut-wrenching scream.

"I . . . I think I know what those are," said Abigail weakly.

"What?" asked Andy.

"Irish folk creatures. My grandmother used to tell me stories. That one in the hat is a Dullahan. It's a headless creature. The short thing with the yellow eyes is a Dearg Due, kind of like a vampire, and the last one . . . she's . . . the Banshee."

"What does the Banshee do?"

Abigail glanced at him nervously. "Her cry means that someone is going to die. If the legends about her are true, she's never, ever wrong."

The creatures had all spotted them now and were moving in their direction.

"I don't know what to do," said Andy despondently. He'd faced many things in his adventures so far, including magically enhanced animals, a mummy, and a Hawaiian god. But ever since he was little, Andy had hated, hated, hated haunted houses and ghosts. He avoided spooky stories and hadn't even enjoyed playing peekaboo as a baby. So seeing three horrible creatures that seemed to have walked straight out of his worst nightmare made his blood turn cold and all courage seem to leave his body.

"Well, we have to think of something," said Abigail

with a panicked tremble in her voice. "They're coming closer!"

The air all around them turned cold as the underworld beings drew closer. Andy felt that these creatures were much different from the monsters he'd already faced. They seemed darker and more sinister.

"I . . . I c-can't . . ." Andy stuttered.

Abigail looked at Andy's terrified expression, then back to the ghouls who were getting closer and closer. "Andy!"

Andy shook himself out of his paralyzing fear. He'd faced a mummy. He could face this! He remembered his father once telling him that true courage was doing what had to be done in spite of feeling afraid. And he was terrified. But he was determined not to let that stop him.

He just couldn't. There was too much at stake!

So when the creatures had come close enough that he could make out the malice in their eyes, Andy raised his pen in a shaking hand and, not entirely sure it would work on ghostly creatures, fired.

KA-THOOOM!

The atomic pulse emitter was fully charged, and the force of its blast ripped all the clawlike tendrils right out of the floor and sent them shooting to the back wall of the cavern like bullets. But because the creatures were supernatural, the blast had little effect upon them. The tendrils shot right through them, and they continued their slow, deadly approach without a pause.

The Banshee got to Andy first and grabbed his arm. The spirit seemed to glow with a sudden burst of eldritch energy. She screeched—a high-pitched, horrible sound—and then, to Andy's surprise, icy pain shot through his forearm.

"*Aaaah!*" he screamed.

Abigail swung at the ghost with her fist. Perhaps it was because the spirit had grown more solid when using her power that the blow connected. The Banshee howled with surprise and let go of Andy's arm.

"Run!" said Abigail, grabbing Andy by the back of his shirt.

Andy didn't need to be told twice. While rubbing his burning arm, he took off after her, running as fast as he could to avoid the ghastly creatures. As he ran, he heard the Banshee's terrible wail once again, but he forced himself to keep moving and tried, as hard as it was, to ignore it.

Chapter Twenty-One
The Three Spirits

There were several organic formations that grew from the root walls and floor, and Andy and Abigail tried to hide by diving behind one of the larger ones. Breathing hard, they looked around the cavern in hopes of seeing a way out, but there didn't seem to be anything other than the tunnel the death carriage had come from. It was directly across from them, with the carriage and horses still halfway inside it.

Abigail saw Andy staring at it and could tell what he was thinking.

"I don't know. . . . If that tunnel is where *they* came from, there could be even worse things waiting for us inside it."

"What other choice do we have?" said Andy, rubbing his sore arm. Looking down at it, he could see claw marks where the spirit had grabbed him.

He glanced back. "Oh, no," he said.

The creatures were reorienting on them and continuing their tireless stalking.

"On the count of three," Andy said. "One . . ."

Abigail didn't wait for *three*. She took off as soon as Andy began counting, and he leapt up and ran after her, too panicked to look behind him.

They raced past the tortured horses and carriage and shot down the dark opening through which they'd come. At first there was some mild relief as they left the cavern, but it was quickly replaced by a feeling of terrible dread.

Out of the frying pan . . . thought Andy as the dark tunnel opened up to an improbable sight. A creeping mist lay low on a crumbling graveyard. Looking up, Andy saw that there was a sickly-looking full moon. He was convinced it was some kind of magical illusion, but it looked so astoundingly real that he could hardly believe his eyes.

"This is impossible," said Abigail.

"Must be leprechaun magic," said Andy. "Come on. We need to find a place to hide before those things get here."

As they darted between the crumbling graves, Andy noticed something out of the corner of his eye: a wooden chest resting on top of a crypt.

Andy's instincts told him that something so out of place couldn't be a coincidence. "Hang on," he said to Abigail. "I need to check something out."

Abigail looked on, confused, as Andy ran over to the small chest. Looking closely at it, he saw that it was engraved with curling script.

I HAVE A HEAD, A TAIL, AND NO LEGS.

Andy stared at the riddle. Abigail, breathing hard from their running, looked over his shoulder.

"Is that a riddle?"

"I think so," said Andy. "But what does it mean?"

Suddenly, another scream from the Banshee split the air. Wheeling around, Andy and Abigail saw the three spirits emerge from the tunnel and continue their advance. The snorting vampire creature with yellow eyes bared its fangs in a vicious grin.

"We've got to hurry!" said Abigail.

"Like I don't know that?" Andy snapped. He quickly added, "Sorry."

Abigail nodded. She was feeling the urgency of the situation, too.

Andy stared at the words, rereading them over and over.

I have a head, a tail, and no legs. I have a head, a tail, and no legs.

"Ah, it's so obvious!" Andy exclaimed. "It's a snake!"

He looked at the chest expectantly, but nothing happened.

"Maybe a fish?"

Still nothing.

"Ugh! This is a tough one!" Andy exclaimed, rubbing his temples in frustration.

It was hard to concentrate when he was panicking. He turned the riddle over and over in his head but couldn't figure out what it might mean.

"I'm not good at riddles. But maybe it has something to do with what's inside the chest?" suggested Abigail hopefully.

"Too obvious . . ." said Andy automatically. But suddenly a thought occurred to him. He wheeled on Abigail with an astonished look. "You're a genius!"

"I am?" said Abigail.

Andy moved close to the chest and said, "A coin."

The lid on the chest suddenly snapped open. Inside was a cache of glittering golden coins.

"Has anyone ever told you that you're really clever?" asked Abigail.

"It was nothing," Andy murmured. He would have blushed at the compliment in any other circumstances, but right now he was too worried to notice. He glanced over his shoulder. The creatures were only thirty yards away.

"Too bad treasure isn't what we need right now. What we need is . . ." But then her eyes widened.

"What is it?" asked Andy.

"I just remembered something!" said Abigail. "My grandma used to say that the Dullahan would flee if given gold coins for a new suit. It never made sense to me then. But it does now!"

Without hesitation, Andy reached inside the chest and retrieved a handful of gold coins. "Think this is enough?" he asked.

"No idea," said Abigail. "But listen, Andy, this is really dangerous. Anybody who gets within ten feet of a Dullahan can be turned into a statue. The trick is not to look him in the eye." Noting the fear on Andy's face and his hesitation, she added, "Do you want me to do it instead?"

"No, that's all right," said Andy. "I've got the coins, and we have no time to argue." Then, gripping the handful of coins tightly in his hand, he ran directly toward the three monsters.

"Be careful!" cried Abigail, aghast.

But Andy didn't reply. As he ran toward the spirits, they suddenly paused, appearing confused. They evidently were not expecting to be confronted directly by the person who was supposed to be their victim!

Andy ran directly at the tall man with no face. It took all his courage to keep his knees from buckling. When he got within ten feet, he shielded his eyes and did his best to visualize where the terrifying creature was hovering.

He cried out, "Dullahan! Here, go buy yourself a new suit!"

And as he threw the gold coins at the tall headless

ghost, the spirit cried out with a terrible shriek! It convulsed as if struck by lightning, shaking and quaking until it faded from view.

Andy turned and kept running, never breaking stride or looking back, as he raced past the other two stunned ghosts and dashed back to Abigail.

"Good work! Now, come on," said Abigail excitedly. "Those stories all scared me half to death. But there's something else I remember."

Andy followed close as they ran between the gravestones. Abigail called to him as they sprinted through the creepy grounds, saying, "We're looking for something called Strongbow's Tree."

"What's that?" asked Andy as he leapt over a low-lying gravestone.

"Should be . . . a large . . . twisted oak," huffed Abigail. She'd been running hard and had beads of sweat stinging her eyes. "Gold . . . destroys the Dullahan. Strongbow's Tree . . . gravesite . . ."

It was all she could muster. But Andy didn't question

her. He ran right beside her, feeling both terrified and relieved that they had some kind of working plan.

Andy spotted the tree. It was a horribly bent and twisted oak tree that had a plain-looking crypt next to its hoary base.

"The legend says . . . the Dearg Due's body . . . was buried at Strongbow's Tree," gasped Abigail, trying to catch her breath. "We . . . have to pile stones on his grave, and then he'll have no choice but to stay in there."

Abigail leapt to the task, and she and Andy searched the area for every stone they could find.

Perhaps it was because the spirits could see that their lives were threatened that they moved more quickly. Andy and Abigail had barely gotten three stones on the crypt when Abigail suddenly let out a cry of pain.

Andy had been so busy looking for rocks that he hadn't seen the vampire spirit sneak up on them. The squat thing had its yellow fangs embedded in Abigail's calf and was sucking at it greedily.

"Get off, you!" shouted Andy. He grabbed the closest

thing he could find, a stout fallen branch from the oak tree, and began frantically clubbing at the creature with all his strength.

The Dearg Due didn't loosen its grip—it clamped down even harder, like a pit bull on a slab of meat. Without thinking about how terrified he was of the monster, Andy gathered all his courage, raised the branch above his head like a knife, and plunged the sharp broken end directly into the creature's back.

And it had a powerful effect. The creature snarled and howled with rage, clawing at the stick that was halfway embedded in its body.

It's just like a stake with a vampire! Andy thought suddenly. While the creature struggled, Andy raced to find enough stones to build a small pyramid of them on the creature's tomb.

The horrible monster was distracted by the wooden stake in its back, giving Andy enough time to complete his task. When Andy had placed the seventh of his gathered stones in the pile of rocks on the granite tomb's lid, the vampire's yellow eyes grew wide with fear.

And then, just like the Dullahan, it slowly faded from view.

Andy rushed to Abigail's side. The young woman was pale and seemed to have lost a lot of blood.

"Can you get up?" asked Andy.

Abigail tried, but then shook her head. "It got me."

Andy was so overcome with anxiety over his friend that he didn't see the spirit that hovered behind him. Abigail's weak gaze lifted to look over his shoulder, and only then did he realize that the Banshee must be there.

"Andy . . ." she whispered.

"I know," said Andy. But he realized that he didn't care. His friend was injured badly, and he was much more concerned about her than anything else.

"What can I do for you?" Andy asked gently. "Does it hurt badly?"

Abigail nodded, her face drawn with pain. As long as he'd known her, Abigail had been one of the toughest people he'd ever met. She was a daredevil who seemed to possess more courage than the entire J.E.S. put together.

Seeing her weak and in such pain was something Andy was hardly prepared for. She was kind of like an older sister to him—beautiful and caring, but not someone who would put up with any nonsense. She was a role model, and he found himself feeling scared at the thought of possibly losing her.

He glanced down, noticing her torn trouser leg and the deep puncture wounds from the vampire's teeth. Andy tore the bottom of his shirttail and wrapped her leg the best he could to try to stop the bleeding.

"Abigail, I . . . I don't know what to do. I don't know where we are or how to get any help," he said. Andy's voice choked with emotion and tears sprang to his eyes. "I wish it had been me instead of you. You . . . you don't deserve this."

Abigail lay pale and unmoving. Her eyes had closed, and he didn't know if she could even hear him.

"Please help her not to suffer. . . . Anything but that . . ."

A single tear dripped off the end of his nose and splashed onto the ground.

Out of the corner of his eye, he caught sight of a shimmer of green light. A voice said, "Begone, spirit."

And the Banshee faded.

Andy felt a small hand on his shoulder.

"You've passed my test. With the riddle on the chest, you've shown cleverness. By facing the spirits, including the Dullahan, you've shown courage, and now, seeing your friend in pain, you've shown nothing but compassion."

Andy couldn't look up, because his eyes were filled with tears. But he was aware of a growing green light that soon seemed to encompass the entire world around him.

And then the graveyard—and Abigail—faded away.

When he opened his eyes, the creature who stood before him reminded Andy of every St. Patrick's Day event he'd ever seen. The little man was dressed exactly like a leprechaun from a storybook, complete with buckled shoes, a tall green hat, and an emerald-colored vest. His impish, bearded face looked at once merry but also ancient and wise.

"The name's Patrick Begorra, and I am the guardian of the Eternal Tree." He smiled gently at Andy and then continued, saying, "Obviously, you both are very persistent youths, or you would have never made it to my door. I try to keep my home well hidden. A tree that grants endless life has been sought after by mortals for generations, but they must know she only bestows that gift to those she feels truly deserve it."

Patrick folded his arms. "People like your sorcerer friend Bungalow Bob have figured out ways to prolong their lives through tapping into her magical roots. The trouble with that is that they are actually stealing from the Eternal Tree. Because their desire is selfish, the magic that prolongs their lives is rooted in selfishness. It might be a long life, but it often isn't a happy one."

"Well, I wouldn't really call Bungalow Bob a friend," said Andy. "As you said, he really only looks out for himself."

Patrick nodded and said, "Just so."

Andy was quiet as he thought about his friends and the battle they were facing. Were they already battling the Potentate's forces? Andy also wondered how Patrick knew so much about them and their mission. Suddenly he thought about Abigail and asked, "Where's my friend? Is she okay?"

"Her wound is very serious, but the chances are good that I can heal her. The bite of the Dearg Due can be fatal. But unlike that of the vampires in Romanian folklore, it doesn't cause the victim to become one of their undead servants."

Andy felt a tiny flicker of hope at the words.

Gazing around, Andy noticed for the first time that he was no longer in the tree's roots. He was standing with Patrick in an immense circular room and realized with some surprise that they must be inside the massive tree's trunk. The polished wooden room was furnished in the fashion of a homey Irish farmhouse, and if it hadn't been for the dire circumstances, Andy would have certainly found it comforting.

"Mr. Begorra, we were sent to ask you a question."

The small man looked up at Andy with a serene expression, as if expecting this. "Ask," he said.

Andy took a deep breath. "An evil woman has activated something called the Doomsday Device. She wants to destroy everyone I care about with it. Please, please, do you know how I can stop her?"

"Yes, Andy Stanley. I do indeed possess the secret to destroying the Doomsday Device. But it isn't what you think it is. In fact, once you discover what it is, you will probably wish you didn't know. But that was the reason for my test. I already knew what you were seeking."

"But how?" asked Andy.

Patrick smiled and gestured to the walls of the Eternal Tree. "She and I go back a long way. I can understand her speech, and her roots are deep, probing into many corners of the earth. The Eternal Tree is always listening and so, in turn, am I."

He gave Andy a serious look. "You love your friends, don't you, Andy Stanley?"

"I'll do anything for them," said Andy firmly. And then he added, with the conviction borne out of seeing one of his closest friends suffering, "Anything."

Chapter Twenty-Two
The Great Artifact War

Andy spent a long time speaking with Patrick Begorra about many mysteries, and during that time he heard several peals of the Doomsday Device's terrible chime. But the things he had to learn from the leprechaun took time to explain. Patrick had to tell him what he knew about the Doomsday Device, how it had been created, and about the heart of the evil sorcerer who had made it in the Middle Ages so that Andy could truly begin to understand the tremendous sacrifice it would take to undo one of the most wicked artifacts ever made.

Andy hadn't really expected the solution to destroying the machine to be as simple as finding a key that could fit inside and stop it. But when he learned of the real "key" it would take to save the lives of his friends, he found that he couldn't speak for several minutes. He just nodded his head as Patrick explained to him that should he do what he had come to do, it was a choice only he could make and no other. After getting a reassurance from Andy that he fully understood what was at stake and still wanted to proceed, the leprechaun began teaching Andy the magic words that would bring about the destruction of the Doomsday Device.

Andy soberly repeated the strange phrase until he had it memorized. The words were ancient and incredibly powerful. And the book Patrick used to teach him the words was a tome even older than the deepest roots of the Eternal Tree. It was a book that had come from the foundations of the world and upon which the world was designed.

And now, here Andy was. He stood on top of a cairn, an ancient burial site for Irish kings, a magical place known now only to the leprechauns, that Patrick had transported him to.

Andy Stanley looked over the battlefield with a solemn purpose in his heart. This would be the most difficult thing he'd ever have to do. But he reassured himself about what he'd been taught and determined to gather his courage and do what he had to.

After repeating the three words that Patrick Begorra had taught him to himself once more, Andy gazed down at the battle that raged in the valley below.

The Collective's army was clothed entirely in black, which made them easy to spot next to the J.E.S. members, many of whom were clothed in safari garb and pith helmets. Others were outfitted in colorful, exotic gear, and Andy assumed from their various cultural dress that they'd come from all corners of the globe. Every nation was represented, and many showed the wear and tear of the various plagues that the Doomsday Device had caused. Andy could see that many looked close to death, and he couldn't help wondering how many had already perished.

In spite of the terrible thing he had to do, Andy felt calm and resolute. Abigail was with Patrick, and Andy was glad that she didn't have to be present for the most deadly battle the J.E.S. had ever been involved with. He hoped that her healing would progress as the leprechaun had promised.

He fingered the juju around his neck, reminding himself to use it if necessary. The key to defeating the Potentate didn't require an artifact of any kind. The secret lay in the three magic words that he now knew and would say at the proper time.

Andy kept repeating the words over and over again as he walked down the hill and toward the fighting. He thought of his friends' faces as he walked, grateful for them and how much they'd brought to his young life.

As the battle drew closer, he tried to find the Potentate among the swarming throngs but had difficulty spotting her. Rare and powerful artifacts were being used all over the place. Some activated colorful magic that shot blazing arcs of fire at their enemy. Others created mythical creatures, hulking dragons and hideous demons that wreaked havoc and laid waste to all who stood in their paths.

Andy glanced to his right and noticed, in the distance, a very haggard Rusty Bucketts, who had just pulled back on his slingshot and let his ball bearing fly at a hulking member of the Collective who was looming over him with an artifact-powered scimitar.

The grizzled giant staggered for a moment and then, like Goliath of old, toppled forward with a ball bearing embedded in his forehead. His glowing sword buried itself in the earth as he collapsed. The scimitar flickered for a moment and then melted into the form of a deadly cobra, slithering off to find an unsuspecting victim among the fighters.

Andy watched as the stalwart Rusty quickly retrieved his shiny eyeball, prying it loose from the giant, and, after wiping it off, popped it back in its socket.

Andy wanted to run over and congratulate his old friend, happily slapping his back as Rusty had done to him more times than he could count. But there wasn't time for that. Patrick had told him that he would have only ten minutes before the Doomsday Device hit its final chime, the one that would kill all the Potentate's enemies in that final fell swoop.

Andy took a deep breath. And then, drawing his Zoomwriter, he let out the loudest shout he could muster and ran headlong into the fray.

Weapons clashed next to his head. Andy ducked. A giant lizard stomped past, its claw missing him by inches. But still he ran, heedless of the danger, searching desperately for the Potentate.

An army of clockwork soldiers outfitted in samurai armor cleared a swath through the crowd, their blades spinning like propellers. Andy fired his Zoomwriter, knocking them back like bowling pins.

And that's when Andy saw her—the Potentate, standing atop a flat piece of rock and holding the Doomsday Device in gloved hands above her head.

Andy took a deep breath. He recited the words once more to keep them firmly in his memory.

And then he ran with all his might directly at his foe.

He raced past the twins, Betty and Dotty, who were spinning and kicking as they sang their eerie war song, a strange melody that was filled with a beautiful, weird harmony that only the sisters could sing. Several of the Collective soldiers fell to their spinning blows in spite of the protective charms they wore around their necks.

Andy dodged an explosive artifact that was tossed to his left. Then he ducked the fist of a giant golem, a stone creature twenty feet tall, to his right. He kept his eyes fixed on his goal: the masked woman on the ledge.

Suddenly, a crowd of evil-looking men and women appeared in front of him. They had surrounded Molly the mime, a member of the J.E.S. and a friend he hadn't seen in ages. The girl was shouting epithets at the top of her lungs at her enemies (she'd never been a very good mime) and casting her juggling knives at them with deadly precision.

But Andy could tell at a glance that she was outnumbered. Without hesitation, he took his juju from his neck and summoned it.

The piranhahaha—a strange, smiling, many-toothed fish—glowed.

As soon as he activated the charm, a laughing fit paralyzed the crowd of soldiers. With tears streaming down their cheeks, they collapsed to the ground.

Molly stared at them in surprise and then caught Andy's eye. She waved an enthusiastic thanks, and Andy gave her a quick wave in return before dashing away.

I only hope that I'll see them all again someday, he thought. *They're the best friends I've ever had.*

But he didn't allow himself to dwell on the task ahead. He knew that if he thought too much about it, he wouldn't have the courage to do what he'd set out to do.

He was glad to see that the Potentate's gaze was focused elsewhere, glued to the skirmish that was happening about twenty or thirty yards from where she stood. Bungalow Bob stood next to a group of J.E.S. members that Andy had seen only briefly at one of the outposts. They fought a group of Collective soldiers led by a roaring Chinese dragon. Andy would have rushed to help them if he could have, but he knew that the time had come.

He started to climb the ledge behind the Potentate, ready to confront his nemesis. But just as he was about to approach his archenemy, he felt something hard punch him in the back, directly between his shoulder blades.

Andy wheeled around and saw the last person standing there that he could ever have expected. Grinning with rows of broken yellow teeth and holding a long, ornately carved lightning rod was none other than Nicodemus Crumb, his wild hair blowing in the wind.

The rod he carried had evidently been the thing Crumb had used to hit Andy in the back, because he pointed it at him and cackled. "Thought you'd gotten rid of me, eh? Thought I'd drowned at sea?" His voice grew menacing. "You, Andy Stanley, have been a boil on my neck since I first laid eyes on you at the funeral. You destroyed my ritual, one that had taken me over a year to produce. I blame you for the wreckage that was once my boat. And I demand from you payment for the pain you've caused me." He spit on the ground before shouting in a wild, enraged voice, "I want those keys, boy—the keys to your grandfather's mansion! They're mine!"

Andy noticed that as his anger grew, dark, heavy storm clouds suddenly began to gather in the sky directly above the old man's head, and a chilly wind blew. Crumb then raised the lightning rod to the heavens and, with his eyes rolled back in his head, began murmuring some kind of spell in a high, whiny voice. It sounded much like the one Andy had heard him attempting at his grandfather's funeral.

Andy reached for his pen. But before he could grasp the Zoomwriter, the lightning rod glowed with a fierce, eerie light, and Crumb, looking like some otherworldly demon with the wind tearing through his long gray hair, pointed his bony finger at Andy.

The next thing Andy knew was the sound of an earth-shattering *CRACK!* as a bolt of white lightning thundered down and stabbed the ground right where Andy stood, completely knocking him off his feet.

Electricity arced around Andy like a Tesla coil, the terrible lightning electrifying his body with tremendous force.

Andy screamed!

As he writhed on the ground, he was dimly aware of

Nicodemus Crumb's high laugh. Then the old man was shouting to a second presence who had arrived beside him, and it was the person Andy loathed and feared more than any other.

The Potentate, alerted by the sudden lightning blast, had joined Crumb. And as the sparking electricity faded away, Andy heard Nicodemus telling her about the keys Andy held and insisting that he deserved a reward for delivering not only the keys but the Keymaster to her as well.

All of this Andy heard as if listening to a faint radio station with poor reception. His ears were thrumming from the blast, and although the electric arcs had stopped sizzling around him, he still felt as if every nerve in his body were jangling.

Whether the Potentate answered Crumb, Andy didn't know. But after Crumb asked the Potentate for compensation, there was a terrible scream, and Andy knew instantly that it was Nicodemus Crumb's voice—and that he was probably dead.

Crumb was the latest victim in the Potentate's campaign of destruction. She didn't need him. Whatever she wanted, she took by force. Andy was in terrible pain, and faint wisps of smoke curled up from his clothing, but when he was able to crack his swollen eyes open, he saw the Potentate with her flowing robes, raven black hair, and deathlike ivory mask peering down at him.

Her head was cocked to one side as if she were considering what she was looking at. Her slim arms were gripping the Doomsday Device, and Andy could see that the minute hand was only a few ticks away from midnight.

Andy knew that when it struck, it would mean the deaths of everyone he loved. That would be it. The entire J.E.S., which had stalwartly resisted every plague the device had delivered and fought to the very end without giving up, would be eliminated.

Then the impact of what he was about to do washed over him. Although he was weak and in terrible pain, something deep inside of him knew that this would be his only chance.

Andy didn't hesitate. Rising up with strength born of conviction, he leapt for the Doomsday Device and grasped it with all his might. A fantastic tug-of-war ensued, with both parties fighting for control of the infernal device.

Andy felt the edges of the deadly artifact pulsing with dark magical power. And right then, the sensation was almost worse than the lightning had been. The terrible, dark energy caused all the muscles in his forearms to seize up, and they seemed to want nothing more than to release the terrible artifact.

But whether that was a magical property of the evil clock or not, Andy didn't know. It didn't matter. He held on in spite of everything the device was throwing at him.

"Let go!" the Potentate shrieked. It seemed that she was experiencing the same discomfort Andy felt. Then, while one hand still held the device, her other darted

One was the Potentate, whose life had ended with the destruction of the terrible clock.

And the other was the youngest Keymaster the Jungle Explorers' Society had ever produced.

Andy Stanley, the grandson of the great Ned Lostmore, was dead.

Chapter Twenty-Three
Endings and Beginnings

The funeral for Andy Stanley was much like the one that had been given for Ned Lostmore—except this time, the person the ceremony was being held for was actually dead.

Ned Lostmore's mansion was half-burned to the ground. True to his prediction, the Potentate had sent several members of the Collective to try to break into his vault of artifacts by force.

It hadn't worked.

Ned had endured every single plague the Doomsday Device had aimed at the Jungle Explorers' Society and had also, with the help of Boltonhouse and Albert Awol, defended the mansion as best as he could. He was pale and ragged, but since the destruction of the Doomsday Device, he and the rest of the Society were on the mend.

It was all thanks to his grandson's sacrifice.

Ned remained inside Boltonhouse's chest in the graveyard by the Lostmore mansion, gazing down at Andy's body, which had been carefully laid on a marble slab. The boy was burned terribly, but his blond hair was neatly combed and he wore a clean outfit of Jungle Explorers' khakis with his favorite leather jacket. His face was pale and his eyes were closed.

Andy's mother and father were also there, looking somber and pale. They seemed stunned by the turn of events, unable to comprehend what had happened to their only son even though it had been explained to them many times. How had their son spending time with his grandfather ended in such tragedy?

Ned stared down at his grandson, his usually bright blue eyes clouded with tears. Other members of the J.E.S.—Rusty Bucketts, Betty, Dotty, Albert Awol, and Molly the mime, each of them bearing the effects of the Great Artifact War—looked ragged but resolute and were standing next to their leader. Below the platform on which they stood were all the other members of the J.E.S. from around the globe, gathered to memorialize the young Keymaster and express their gratitude for his tremendous sacrifice.

"My friends," began Ned, "there are no words to express what we are all feeling here today. Andy Stanley, my grandson, has embodied through his actions the greatest qualities that any member of our society could aspire to. He has shown courage and loyalty beyond question and has, to all who knew him, been an inspiration, a true and beloved friend."

Betty and Dotty both sniffled. Even Rusty Bucketts wiped his eye and blew his nose on his pocket handkerchief.

"The loss that we've all experienced is one that can never be undone. But it is my honor as the head of the J.E.S. to bestow upon Andy Stanley, my grandson, the highest honor that we possess: the Golden Toucan, for outstanding courage, unending loyalty, compassion without measure, and fortitude in the face of the gravest dangers."

Boltonhouse moved forward. Several people were crying openly as they watched Ned pin the medal on his grandson's chest.

Andy Stanley's loss, for many, was incomprehensible.

Nobody at the funeral, not even the great Ned Lostmore, knew what was going on deep underground. And when tiny root tendrils sprouted from the ground and grew slowly up around Andy's body, most of those gathered were too overcome with grief to notice. Like probing vines, the roots rose up around Andy's arms and legs, and wherever they touched him, small white flowers sprouted.

Then, after the vines had found their position, they began to glow with a very faint green light. Where the roots and tendrils touched Andy's body, the essence of life flowed from within them and then magically transferred directly to his pale, unmoving body.

Which was why, when Andy's eyes suddenly flickered open, many who hadn't been able to conceive of living life without him were rewarded with never having to consider that option again.

A gasp spread through the crowd as color returned to the boy's cheeks. Then a brief magical glow appeared, radiating like a halo around him before fading away. The roots that had gently enclosed his wrists and feet withdrew slowly back into the nutrient-rich ground.

Andy knew, as he saw them disappear, exactly what

had happened to him. He could almost hear Patrick Begorra in his mind, telling him again about the roots of the world's oldest living creature and how they extended under the earth, going farther and deeper than anyone knew. Patrick had also told him that the tree was always listening. He'd said that she gave her most precious gift only when she chose to do so.

And to Andy's immense surprise, the Eternal Tree had given him that gift—the one that all who sought to find her wanted more than anything else.

Life.

And he hadn't even asked for it, nor expected it back when he'd made his greatest sacrifice.

Andy blinked and stared around. Sitting up from the slab upon which he'd been recently laid to rest, he felt like he'd had the best sleep of his life. All his burns and bruises were gone, and health seemed to radiate from every one of his pores. The others gazed at him in disbelief, unable to comprehend what they were seeing.

Then, noticing where he was and what was happening, Andy laughed with joy. He noticed his friends' and family's shocked expressions and grinned. Then Ned Lostmore, with the help of Boltonhouse, rushed over and embraced his grandson. Being hugged by a robot wasn't a particularly comfortable thing to experience, but the tears of joy streaming down his grandfather's face behind the glass in Boltonhouse's chest made Andy feel warm inside.

"My boy! You're alive!"

Andy nodded. "Thanks to the Eternal Tree," he said. "She was the one who gave me back my life."

"She?" asked Ned. Then he gazed into his grandson's eyes and saw a new kind of wisdom there, something that came from having journeyed to the place of mankind's deepest fear—death itself—and returned.

"Thunderation! I guess that blasted tree was good for something after all!" shouted Rusty happily.

Everyone cheered! Andy blushed. His mother and father rushed over, kissing him and embracing him in fierce hugs. Andy held on tight. After they let go, the reality of having her son back after nearly losing him forever must have struck Andy's mother, for she suddenly burst into happy tears.

Andy squeezed his mother's shoulders. Then he glanced down at his chest and noticed, for the first time, the gleaming medal that was pinned there.

"What's this?" he asked.

"The greatest honor the Jungle Explorers' Society has to offer," said Ned, smiling.

Comprehension and awe washed over Andy's face. "You mean I'm actually a full member of the J.E.S.?"

"And then some," chimed in Betty and Dotty simultaneously.

Andy had never felt better in his life! And when that thought occurred to him, he couldn't help laughing at the thought that followed.

The best I've ever felt in both my previous life and my new one!

Everyone cheered and patted Andy on the back.

What had been a funeral suddenly turned into the biggest party the Jungle Explorers' Society had ever had. Andy's happiness was magnified one hundred times when someone came walking up to him with a big, beaming smile on her face.

"Abigail!" Andy shouted. He rushed over to the girl and threw his arms around her. "When did you get here?"

"Just now," she laughed, hugging Andy back. She pointed to the edge of the crowd, where remnants of faint green smoke were dissolving into the air.

"Patrick?"

Abigail nodded. "Leprechauns have an amazing way of getting around! He promised that I'd be completely back to normal in a few more days. But when I heard what had happened to you, I had to come right away."

"I'm glad you did," said Andy, his eyes shining. Abigail looked a little pale and was leaning on a wooden cane for support, but she seemed far better than she had when he'd left her.

Albert and the others caught sight of Abigail and came running. As Abigail's father shouted with glee and wrapped her in an enormous but gentle bear hug, the others also surrounded her with a million questions each about what had happened to her under Patrick Begorra's care.

Andy grinned at the happy scene and walked a little away from the crowd, relishing the moment. It felt nice to have the attention diverted away from himself so he could think about all that had happened to him.

He gazed down at his hands and flexed his fingers. It was good to be alive!

He thought about all that he'd been through, and it was hard to believe where he'd started. He'd come so far from the introverted, scared little boy he'd been before meeting his grandfather and joining the J.E.S.

At the edge of the grassy lawn, he stared up at the sky, noticing the twinkling stars above and appreciating them in a whole new way. Having died and returned brought a certain perspective to everything. The moonlight reflected on his new medal, and he truly felt like anything was possible.

Adventures are funny things, he thought. *You can read about them in books, and they seem exciting. But until you go out there and truly experience them for yourself, nothing can really prepare you for how much they change you. They're sometimes scary and sometimes dangerous, but in the end they are what make you feel truly alive.*

He was lost in thought for a while and felt that he could have gone on staring at the heavens for much longer, but the moment was interrupted when he heard the others calling his name. He turned and saw his friends beaming at him and motioning him over. Andy smiled back at them and then, after one more glance at the night sky, ran back over the dewy grass, feeling very happy that he could enjoy all the sensations life had to offer.

As he ran to his friends, he tried to think of a word that could describe how he was feeling, both proud and ready for anything that life could throw at him.

And then the perfect word came to him, and he couldn't help hollering it as he ran back to the crowd of the dearest people he'd ever known. He shouted it at the top of his lungs, a joyful cry that seemed to embody all the happiness that was welling up inside of him like a roaring, tumbling fountain.

"Kungaloosh!"